THE JINDABYNE SECRET

DROWNED EARTH

DROWNED EARTH

Eight novellas.
Eight Australian authors.
One watery apocalypse.

Scientists said that it would take 5000 years for Earth's oceans to rise.

They were wrong.

After an asteroid collides with Antarctica, a tsunami devastates the world's coastal cities and escalates the melting of the ice caps.

These eight novellas set in various locations around Australia explore the potential consequences of such a catastrophe. They can be read in any order.

Prequel short story: Shards of Silver by Alanah Andrews
The Rise by Sue-Ellen Pashley
Fire Over Troubled Water by Nick Marone
Submerged City by Austin P. Sheehan
Tides of War by Marcus Turner
The Jindabyne Secret by Jo Hart
River of Diamonds by S. M. Isaac
Salvaged by C.A. Clark
Emoto's Promise by Shel Calopa

THE JINDABYNE SECRET

JO HART

DROWNED EARTH

DEDICATION

To my children: William, Stephanie, Kate and Zachary.

In hopes I can leave them a better world than the one depicted in these pages.

CHAPTER ONE

Jax pressed the steel flask to his dry, cracked lips and tipped it slowly, letting the smallest trickle wet his parched throat. Still thirsty, he put the flask back on the highest shelf. There were only five bottles left, and though each flask stood as tall as his forearm and as wide as a fence post—holding five litres when full—it wasn't enough.

It was never enough.

The heat wrapped around him like a suffocating blanket as he returned outside to finish his chores. A lone goat stood by a concrete trough bleating. They'd once had a herd of about twenty, but no rain meant no feed. And no feed meant no goats.

"Hold on, Missy, old girl. I'm coming," Jax said, hauling himself over the fence.

The blazing sun glinted on the solar panel above the pump causing Jax to squint as he switched it on. The ancient motor rattled and grumbled into life. Seconds later, mud brown water sloshed into the trough. The goat stuck her nose directly into the spray, shaking her head and snorting when it splashed into her nostrils. The smell of the water infiltrated Jax's senses, calling out to him. Tempting him. He yearned to stick his head in the trough and lap it up, but knew all too well that the resulting three days of stomach cramps and diarrhoea would only dehydrate his body more. Good thing Missy had a cast-iron stomach—what was left of her stomach, anyway. The poor beast was barely more than a skeleton these days. How much longer until he would have to pull out his father's old shotgun? Jax felt sick at the thought. She'd been a good goat. She'd given them milk longer than any of the others. If his father was still alive, he would have killed her the moment she dried up and used her for meat while she still had some on her bones.

But Jax couldn't do it. He couldn't bear the thought of her trusting brown eyes staring up at him as he ended her life. There was too much death already. The only other option was to take her to the market where he might be able to trade the old girl for some hydro canisters. He probably wouldn't get much water for her—not in her condition—but he might get enough to help his family survive until the next ration drop. That's if Tavai hadn't raised his prices again.

"Risked me life to source these hydro canisters," he'd said last time Jax had been desperate enough to make a trade. "Can't be selling them for nothing."

I might as well go ask, Jax thought. *At least find out if it's worth bringing her in to trade.*

***

The marketplace bustled with traders hawking their wares—things they'd pilfered from the old settlements or pitiful vegetables that demanded a high price. Jax pushed through the throng of people milling around the stalls bartering their meagre possessions. Tavai's stall usually sat near the eastern end of the market, but today it wasn't there.

"You looking for Tavai, kid?" called an old man from the stall opposite. His liver-spotted head reminded Jax of the speckled eggs in the nest his little sister Nell had pulled down from the old gum last week. They'd all proclaimed Nell a hero when she discovered them—they hadn't had eggs since the last of their chickens died months ago.

Jax approached the ramshackle booth crammed full of electrical odds and ends. "Yeah" he said. "You seen him? I was hoping to talk to him about a trade."

The old man's face puckered and he shook his head. "They got him."

"Who got him?"

"The gov'ment o'course. What'd he expect? Stealin' hydro canisters. It was only a matter o' time before they caught him."

A frown creased Jax's forehead. "What will they do to him?"

The man laughed humourlessly. "Doncha know the penalty for stealin' water?"

Jax shook his head.

"Firin' squad."

"They killed him?" Jax's head reeled. Tavai was dead. Tavai whose wide grin had been a familiar sight at the market for as long as he could remember, who always had a joke to share, and who gave Jax the best trades.

The old man shrugged. "Water's a precious resource. The gov'ment don't stand for anyone takin' more'n their fair share."

Jax brushed a shaking hand through his hair. The idea that Tavai had been killed—by the government no less, the same government who gave them monthly rations—was hard to fathom.

"You all right, kid?" the old man asked.

"Yeah." Jax balled his hands into fists to stop them shaking. "I just didn't expect it, you know? Tavai is—was—one of those guys that seemed invincible."

The old man pursed his lips and nodded.

They both stood silently for a moment. Tavai. Dead. Jax was used to death. Death was part of life out in the settlements. People died every day from dehydration, from the heat, from starvation. The day Jax's own father died would be forever burned into his memory—the way he lay there like a skeleton under that thin blanket, rasping for breath before his chest stopped rising and falling altogether.

But there was something unsettling about the way Tavai had died. For his life to have been purposefully taken from him by other humans—humans who were supposed to look after people—seemed extra cruel. Mother Nature took enough lives every day, what right did the government have to add to that body count? Shouldn't they be trying to preserve as many lives as possible?

The old man's voice broke through Jax's thoughts. "You were lookin' for a trade?"

"Yeah," said Jax, pulling himself out of his reverie. "I don't suppose you know anyone else who trades canisters?"

"Nah, too dangerous. Tavai was the only one crazy enough to risk it." The man lowered his voice, leaning in closer to Jax. "But if it's water you want, I can help. Name's Ollie." He held out his hand and Jax shook it.

"How can you help me if you don't trade hydro canisters?" Jax scrutinised the shelves of wires and metal gizmos.

"I got somethin' better." Ollie glanced around to make sure no-one was paying them any attention. He pulled out a scrap of paper from under the counter, scrawled down some words with an old stub of a pencil, and handed it to Jax.

"What's this?" asked Jax, glancing at the address written on the paper.

"It's me house. Come over t'night after sundown." Ollie fixed Jax with a steely gaze. "And don't let no-one see ya."

***

The ramshackle hut stood at the end of a long dirt track hidden by a row of lifeless trees standing like grey ghosts that cast long, black, clawed shadows across the ground. Old sheet iron and odd pieces of wood formed the exterior of the house. Jax wondered if Ollie had built it himself. Faded green paint peeled from a front door that barely clung to its hinges.

Jax knocked sharply three times as Ollie had instructed. Lightning flashed in the distance, stark and bright against the dark sky, followed by the rumble of thunder. He lifted his nose and inhaled, hoping for that tell-tale hint of rain, but the air smelled as dry as ever. With any luck, the lightning wouldn't start any fires nearby.

The door opened slowly and the barrel of a shotgun peeked through the gap.

Jax stepped backwards. "It's just me," he said with a nervous laugh and a slight quaver to his voice. "Ollie, it's Jax."

The door opened wider. Ollie appeared framed in the darkness, shotgun in hand. Jax wondered what he was getting himself into.

"Can't be too careful," Ollie said, inclining his head towards the gun in his hand. "Damn poachers'll wipe ya clean."

Jax gave a curt nod, his rapidly beating heart slowing back to normal.

"Come in." Ollie motioned for Jax to follow him into the hut.

Stepping inside, Jax half expected to find a stockpile of hydro canisters. Instead, the single-room hut was crammed full of electrical bits and pieces, mechanical parts, and random odds and ends like Ollie's market stall. Amongst the piles of junk Jax could just make out a bed and a small kitchen. He studied the various gizmos and gadgets—most of which he had no idea of the original purpose—as Ollie shuffled around in one of the kitchen drawers.

"I know I put it in 'ere somewhere," Ollie muttered, rattling about. "Ah, got it."

He emerged from the drawer with a yellowed piece of paper. "Tavai gave it to me ages ago in case anythin' happened to him 'n' I needed to get water for meself," Ollie said, holding the furled paper out to Jax.

"What is it?" Jax raised an eyebrow.

"It's a map," said Ollie, pushing it into Jax's hands.

"A map to what?"

"To water, o' course."

"But the river's all dried up. Everyone's dams are empty," Jax said, confused. "Is there a secret underground spring or something?"

Ollie shook his head. "It's a map to the gov'ment's water facility."

Jax's first instinct was to push the map back into Ollie's hands, but he stood frozen, unable to make his arm cooperate with his brain.

"I'll never use it," continued Ollie. "Got a bung leg 'n' arthritis in me hands. If Tavai got caught, what hope have I got gettin' in. But you…" Ollie eyed Jax up and down. "A spry young fella like you. You'd get in 'n' out no worries."

Jax finally managed to regain control of his body and tentatively took the map from Ollie's hand, staring at the spot marking the facility. "A map to the government water facility? Are you crazy?"

"You wan' it, though. Don't ya? I can already see the thirst in ya eyes."

"How do I even know if this map is real?" Jax asked, trying not to show Ollie he was right—holding that map felt like holding the most precious treasure in the world. Water was life. "It could lead me to the middle of nowhere for all I know."

"I can assure ya it's fair dinkum. But if you don't believe me, you can always go have a gander for yerself. You got nothin' to lose jus' by lookin'."

"You don't even know me," said Jax, his head spinning. "Why give something this valuable to a complete stranger?"

"I know Tavai liked ya," Ollie said casually, licking his lips. "O'course nothin' comes for free. It's quite valuable, as you say, but I'm an old man 'n' it is worth nothin' sittin' in me kitchen drawer. As repayment for sharin' the map, you'll bring me back water. Fifty-fifty."

"I have six mouths needing water, you have just one," Jax pointed out. "And I would be the one taking all the risk."

Ollie chuckled. "Tavai said you're a good negotiator. Alrigh', seventy per cent for you 'n' thirty per cent for me. Sound fair?"

Jax almost said yes.

"No, I can't do it." He tried to hand the map back to Ollie. "I've got a mother and four little sisters to take care of; I can't go getting myself killed."

"If you was tryin' to trade with Tavai, you gotta be desperate for water. You got little sisters, you say? You gonna be able to live with yerself when they dyin' o' thirst, knowin' you coulda helped 'em?" He pushed the map back towards Jax. "Take it, kid. Think about it. Mull over it for a week 'n' if you really don't wanna do it, then bring the map back 'n' I'll find someone else who's willin' to make a deal. Plenty o' people out there desperate for water. But like I said, Tavai liked ya. I reckon he'd have wanted it to be you."

Jax made a last attempt to hand the map back to Ollie, but the old man waved him away. "One week."

***

Jax hardly slept that night. Every now and then he slipped out of bed, pulled the yellowed map from its hiding place beneath his mattress, and held it up so the moonlight gleaming through his window illuminated the inky black line showing the way to the water facility.

"Lake Jindabyne," Jax murmured, running his finger over the words. He checked the scale and measured the distance with his fingers. It was closer than he thought it would be. Had it really been within reach all this time? No one ever left the settlement, so he supposed it wasn't really surprising that no one had known it was there. Except for people like Tavai who was more daring than most. The hydro canisters always came in by chopper, so Jax had assumed the water came from somewhere far away.

He stared at the line showing an old road running from New Wulgulmerang to Lake Jindabyne. If he could get his dad's old solar truck running it would take him less than a day to get there and back. But what if he got caught and killed? His mum wasn't going to last much longer if she didn't stop giving up her water rations to Jax's sisters, and then they would be left with no-one.

Marn, the eldest of his sisters, was barely sixteen and completely hopeless with practical stuff like fixing fences and growing crops. In another life, back in the old world Jax's mother sometimes talked about, she might have been a dancer or an artist—something creative and delicate. She was not cut out for the labour required to run a farm and keep the family from perishing. The others were all too young.

Jax could not afford to be executed. He was crazy to even consider stealing hydro canisters.

He hastily folded the map and shoved it back under his mattress, out of sight.

CHAPTER TWO

Jax held the hydro canister to Annika's mouth and tipped it gently. Her frame was so small that the canister was nearly as big as her entire torso. The tiny girl gulped down the precious liquid. One. Two. Three gulps.

"That's enough, Annika," Jax said, pulling away the flask and screwing the lid back on.

Annika's wide brown eyes pleaded for more, but she didn't say a word. Even at five years old she knew that water had to be carefully rationed and there was no point arguing about it.

"Go play, Annika," Jax urged.

"It's too hot."

"Then go lay under that bark humpy Nell made yesterday."

Annika pouted and crossed her arms. "Nell says I'm not allowed in because it's hers."

"We'll see about that." He swung Annika onto his back and galloped her outside to an old dry creek bed, where a crude, little hut had been made from pieces of bark and twigs.

"Nell," Jax called, as he lowered Annika to the ground.

An eye peeked out from a gap in the bark. "I'm not Nell," came a voice from inside the humpy.

"Then who are you?"

The girl lowered her voice into a deep growl. "I'm the bunyip of Boggy Creek."

"A bunyip? And I suppose, bunyip of Boggy Creek, that this is your house?"

"Yes it is," the bunyip girl growled. "And annoying little sisters are not allowed in unless they want to be gobbled up."

"See," Annika said, lip quivering, "she won't let me in."

"Well we certainly don't want you to be gobbled up by a bunyip. There's only one solution."

"What?"

"We'll just have to build you a humpy of your own."

Jax set Annika to work collecting bits of bark and

twigs while he started building.

A little face with two scraggly plaits belonging to a nine-year-old girl poked out from the bunyip's humpy to watch.

Jax made a show of placing the bark so that it fell down into a messy pile. "I just wish we could make it as good as the bunyip's humpy," he said. "But I can't get this bark to stand up. I wonder if that bunyip could give us some pointers."

The rest of the girl's skinny body emerged and she marched over to her big brother. "Well for starters, you've got to make a frame."

Jax winked at Annika as Nell dragged over two sticks and started putting them together.

As the three of them worked, another girl came skipping down to the creek. She wore plaits like Nell and her cut off denim shorts exposed her knobbly knees. The past few months she'd had a growth spurt, giving her the appearance of a gangly gum tree.

"Hi Yara," Annika said. "We're building a humpy just for me."

"Can I help, too?" the older girl asked, then ran off to collect bark without waiting for an answer.

With Yara's swift bark collecting, they made short work of putting the humpy together.

"Look, I'm a bunyip, too!" Annika said, crawling

inside.

"You can be my next-door-neighbour bunyip," Nell said, and gave a roar.

"I can be the human you try to eat," Yara said. "But you'll never catch me." She sprinted off to the nearest tree and swung herself up into the branches before her little sisters could catch her. Jax watched them play. It wasn't all bad, he thought, not if his sisters could still have fun.

A fourth girl came to stand by Jax—at sixteen she looked more woman than girl these days, though he would always consider her his baby sister.

She gave him a playful punch on the shoulder. "Remember when we used to play like that."

Jax scruffed her hair, which he knew she hated. "If it isn't the mysterious Marn. What brings you out of your cave—I mean room?"

She rolled her eyes at him. "Mum says to come up to the house for lunch."

"I'll round up the ferals." Jax gave a shrill whistle. "Last one to the house is a goat turd."

Marn gave him a reproachful look. "You shouldn't teach them stuff like that."

"Why?" Jax asked.

"It's not ladylike." She turned and started back towards the house.

The sad truth was that there was no room in this world for ladies—the kind that Marn so desperately wanted to be. Better to be rough and tough like the other girls.

Yara zoomed past her and Annika followed behind with her five-year-old legs pumping hard to keep up. Nell walked, coughing and wheezing from over-exertion.

Jax frowned—his sister's cough was worse than yesterday. The haze of smoke from a distant bushfire had been playing havoc with her asthma all week.

"Come on, squirt, I'll piggy back you," he said, kneeling so she could climb on.

"Don't call me squirt," Nell said between wheezes as she gripped her arms around his neck.

"Reckon we can beat Marn?"

"She's as good as a fresh goat turd."

***

After lunch Jax made sure his sisters all took a few sips of water before shooing them back out to play in the humpies. As Annika disappeared out the door after her older sisters, Jax returned the steel flask to the shelf. The temperatures had soared to forty degrees every day for two weeks now. The next government chopper wouldn't arrive to hand out water rations until next Friday. His thoughts flickered to the map hidden under his mattress, but he just as quickly dismissed it. It had been nearly a week since Ollie had handed it to him. Ollie expected the map back the following day if Jax chose not to use it and he fully intended on giving it back.

His mother came in through the door, her arms full of withered turnips from the garden. Her skin was as dry and wrinkled as paperbark and her dark hair hung limply around her gaunt face.

"If only we could bottle sweat and drink it," she said, dumping the turnips on the bench and taking off her dusty boots. "I could fill a whole tank."

Jax took the half-empty flask back down and held it out to her.

She didn't take it. "How much is left?"

"Half in this one and one full one. About seven and a half litres altogether."

"Save it for the girls."

"You need to drink, too."

"I'm going to lie down."

Jax watched her shuffle off down the dark hallway, the neck of the flask still grasped in his outstretched hand. He slammed it down onto the bench and stormed out the door into the stifling air outside. His father had been stubborn, too, forgoing his own share of the rations to make sure his wife and children had enough, and look what happened to him!

Jax paid little attention to where he was going, kicking at rocks and breaking branches from trees as he walked past. He could see the big tree in the distance under which his father's grave stood and he hastily looked away. Finally he stopped and took several deep breaths to calm himself. He found himself in the back corner of their large and unkept yard. In front of him, with brown weeds entangling the tyres, stood a half-rusted truck. The truck had been built by Jax's father from old car parts and pieces of scrap metal. Jax recalled sitting outside in the dusty yard under the shade of the old gum tree watching his father work on it, a hundred flies sitting on the back of his tattered grey singlet.

Jax had watched enough to have a fairly decent idea of how the truck worked and now he examined it more closely. The tyres, though tangled with weeds, seemed to be in good nick. They could do with a bit of air, but they should get him from New Wulgulmerang to Lake Jindabyne and back. The solar panels were still attached. A look under the hood and an initial examination of the engine gave Jax hope.

He spent the rest of the day pulling out weeds, tightening the screws on the solar panels, tinkering with the engine and pumping up the tyres. At last, when Jax turned the key in the ignition, the engine emitted a low hum. The sound stirred up memories of driving lessons with his father years ago.

"That's it, Jax, gently on the accelerator. It's a touchy old thing, doesn't take much and you'll be airborne."

Jax did a few laps of the paddock. Despite the years since he last drove her, all her quirks started coming back to him. The touchy accelerator, the way the steering veered to the left, and how the gearstick always needed a bit of a jiggle when moving it from first to second.

He'd missed the feel of being behind the wheel. They hadn't had much use for the truck in New Wulgulmerang and parts were getting harder and harder to come by. Most of the community was in walking distance and no one bothered trying to leave—what was the point? The government did water ration drops every few weeks, so it was better to stay and be guaranteed water, than venture out and be stuck with none. Even on the coast, Jax had heard rumours of tainted water sources and harsh conditions.

After the Rise and the increased extreme weather, inland Australia had become dry and ravaged by bushfires. New Wulgulmerang sat in a pocket that managed to get just enough rain to sustain the land, though who knew how long that would last as the rains came less and less these days. So far they'd been lucky when it came to bushfires, though there had been a few close calls. A good thing, too, because the truck wouldn't have got them anywhere in a hurry tangled up in weeds.

Jax slowed to a stop, turned off the engine and rested his head on the steering wheel. He couldn't leave his family and risk his life. Not even for water.

The passenger door opened. Jax looked up to see Nell climbing into the seat beside him.

"You got it working," she said, an excited glint in her eye.

"Yeah, I got it working."

"Can you take me for a ride?"

Jax chuckled. "Sure thing. Seatbelt on."

Nell squealed with delight as Jax hooned around the paddock, the way his father had done with him all those years ago, throwing up dust behind them. He only stopped when Nell started coughing. He parked the truck once more, looked over at Nell and studied her gaunt, freckled face.

Between coughs she flashed him a toothy grin. "That was ace, can we go again?"

"You need to have a break," Jax said, unclipping the seatbelt for her. "When was the last time you had some water?"

"I dunno, just after lunch, I guess."

"Go have a few sips."

After she'd run off to the house, coughing all the way, Jax rested his head against the steering wheel again. In his heart he knew there was no way those canisters would last until the next ration drop.

***

I must be insane, Jax thought the following morning. Though the sun had not yet risen, a cock crowed from the neighbour's farm. Jax tucked the note he had scrawled to his mother between the dusty salt and pepper shakers on the worn kitchen table. With a pack full of supplies on his back and his father's old Akubra on his head, he took one deep breath and blew it out before tiptoeing out the door.

CHAPTER THREE

The truck bumped along the dirt track. The smell of eucalyptus filled Jax's nostrils and magpies warbled 'good morning'. Everyone still slept inside their houses, though Jax knew it wouldn't be long until they started to stir. Even the usually busy market stood still and quiet. In a few hours the stall holders would set up for the day and trading would begin. Ideally Jax would have preferred to travel at night away from the heat of the day, but he didn't entirely trust the solar to run without direct sunlight; he wasn't sure how well the battery stored power after being out of use so long.

By the time Jax left the refugee village, the sun peeked above the horizon, casting a golden glow upon the mountains in the distance. The mountains had been the beacon that had drawn the refugees towards them when the waters rose—a promise of higher ground and safety. His parents had been among those seeking salvation. They had told him the story.

It began with the sea waters rising, but fleeing the coastal cities and migrating to higher ground was only the beginning of their problems. The temperatures climbed ever higher at an alarming rate. And while the coast may have been flooded by sea water, fresh water was harder to come by. More heat equalled less rainfall. Less rainfall equalled less water in the rivers and lakes. Lush, fertile areas turned to desert. People who survived the initial flooding, died in the thousands in this new climate. Those who were left, faced another problem: food. Crops withered. Animals died. The Earth faced mass extinction, but Jax's family and the others in their mountain settlement still clung to survival. To hope.

Jax had never known the world before the Rise. He'd been born twelve months later when the New Wulgulmerang settlement was still in its infancy. Most of the babies born around that time had not survived. Some had even been subject to mercy killings, as fear and panic about a bleak future took hold of the survivors. Better to be killed as a baby than face a life of suffering. Jax had beaten the odds and so had his sisters in the years that followed. His father had always said their family was built tough. Built to survive. But it didn't matter how tough you were when you had no water. Even the tough will die of thirst, though they might last a little longer than some. His father had been proof of that. The image of his father's weak and failing body haunted Jax's dreams.

The sun rose higher and the temperature soared. Another scorcher of a day. It was a dizzying kind of heat—the kind that made the air look blurry—and even with the windows wound fully down, the hot air blowing through them made no difference to the temperature inside the truck. The small fan on the dash struggled to turn—stopping and starting in spurts and stutters. The minimal breeze it blew into Jax's face did not prevent the sweat from trickling down his forehead and into his eyes. Like the little fan, Jax felt his thoughts stopping and starting. Like the fan, he didn't know how much longer he could go on before he would have to stop. He hadn't dared to take any water with him, leaving it for his family in case he couldn't get back before it ran out—or in case he didn't come back at all. He couldn't think about that, though, or his nerves might fail him.

Jax tried to wet his parched mouth with non-existent saliva, probing his dry, cracked lips with the tip of his tongue. The tangy taste of sweat rested in the creases. One of the traders at the market, a man named Salim, had told Jax stories of being a salvager on the coast after the Rise—of how he would dive for treasure in the drowned ruins of the cities. He had described to Jax the salty taste of the sea. Jax could almost imagine it: the wavering air in front of him like the waves of the ocean, the salty taste on his tongue, the abandoned factories on the roadside like the drowned ruins of the coastal cities full of treasures to salvage…

A stutter in the engine brought him back to the present and he jerked the steering wheel to avoid the oncoming tree. Heart pounding, he straightened up on the road. The engine gave another stutter and Jax hoped the truck wouldn't give up on him. For that matter, he hoped his own body would hold up. The map fluttered on the dash where he had pinned it down with a rock. As far as he could tell the government facility shouldn't be too much farther. He guessed he'd been driving for about three hours already, judging by the position of the sun. He glanced at the watch on his wrist—the watch that had once belonged to his father—to confirm. It should only take him another hour to get to Lake Jindabyne, if his rough estimations were accurate.

The old road passed through burnt-out towns that once teemed with people, before they were ravaged by bushfires. Burnt bushland always found a way to regrow, but not so with burnt towns. Buildings stood blackened and crumbled; a stark reminder of an Australia that no longer existed.

Jax drove for long stretches on roads that cut into steep hillsides or wound and turned alongside an old, dry river bed. It must have once been a mighty river. Now not even a trickle remained to wet his parched tongue and wisps of breeze blew up the dust from the phantom river's rocky bottom.

The landscape gradually changed. Green instead of brown. It smelled different here. Jax couldn't quite put his finger on it. There was something about the air that wasn't so dry or stifling. A tall concrete wall rose up before him, with barbed wire adorning the top in razor-sharp spirals. Jax's heart jumped into his throat. He had half-expected the facility not to exist, for the map to have been a lie. It felt strangely surreal to have actually found it. He parked the truck behind the tree line and dragged over some fallen leafy branches to cover it. The ground beneath his feet felt softer than he was used to, almost springy.

The map on the dash included a scrawled note in the bottom corner instructing Jax to follow the wall until he found a broken section; this would allow him to access the facility. Clutching half a dozen cannisters to his chest, Jax circled the wall, searching for the opening. The concrete seemed to go on forever—impenetrable and foreboding. Twice he thought he'd found the entry point in places where the wall crumbled, but the concrete only gave the illusion of a hole; behind the crumbling concrete was nothing but more concrete. Jax began to wonder if the opening still existed. Perhaps when Tavai had been caught, the government had repaired the wall to prevent further intruders.

Just as he thought he ought to give it up for a lost cause and head back home, Jax came to a part of wall that had crumbled away to leave a narrow gap—just wide and high enough for an average-sized man to squeeze through. Jax, as skinny as he was, wouldn't even need to squeeze.

Tentatively he poked his head through to see if the coast was clear, fully expecting a soldier with a gun to be standing on the other side. But there didn't appear to be any immediate sign of human life apart from a row of quiet houses in the distance. His immediate thought was that the map had been wrong after all and that this was just another settlement or an old abandoned town where Tavai scavenged for things to trade. Jax hunched down, the canisters cradled in his arms, and stepped through the gap, grazing his shoulder on the concrete. Standing on the other side of the wall he gasped. It was an entirely different world. A cacophony of sounds overwhelmed his ears—a million insects buzzing, pretty bird songs high in the trees and an unfamiliar *croak croak*. In front of him lay a massive body of water. Not a brown pond that might have formed after the rain, but miles of clear blue water—more water than he even knew existed. A breeze blew across the lake rippling the surface. It shimmered and glittered in places where the sun shone upon it. Jax had never seen water so blue—as blue as the sky above it. Long white clouds sat low above the treetops on the opposite bank and reflected in the water like a mirror. Where the water lapped against the bank it made a rhythmic whooshing sound.

Jax moved closer to it, mesmerised. Here and there birds chirped and squawked in the trees—more birds than he had ever seen together all at once, like it was some kind of bird meeting place. A large white bird with a long neck flew low over the water to scoop up a feast in its bill, leaving white frothy waves in its wake. Jax fell to his knees at the water's edge, letting the canisters tumble onto the grass at his side, and bent down to lap at the water like an animal, slurping it in and relishing the cool moist feel running down his throat. It was pure bliss.

When he had drunk his fill, Jax splashed some water over his face and body, then he knelt there taking it all in, wondering if there was some way to bring his mother and sisters here—though he knew it would be too dangerous. And yet... so far he had seen no sign of human life. Could Ollie have been telling tall tales, assuming the worst because Tavai had never returned? Maybe Tavai was in one of those houses in the distance, enjoying the good life instead of returning to the settlement where every day was another step closer to dehydration and death.

A mob of kangaroos bounded close, surrounding Jax and ignoring him as they munched and tore at the grass, heads bent low, bums in the air. The roos in the bush near Jax's home were skinny and scraggly, but these roos were plump with smooth sleek fur. A joey poked its head out of its mother's pouch.

All at once several of the roos put their heads up curiously, ears pricked, as though they had heard something Jax had not. Without warning those closest to him scattered, bounding away at top speed. Jax swung around to see what had spooked them. All he saw was a fist right before it punched him in the face.

CHAPTER FOUR

Jax opened his eyes. Gradually, he became aware that he was laying on his back in grass that tickled his skin. Something stood over him, so he blinked to refocus. A kangaroo's furry nose sniffed at his face, observing him with big brown eyes.

"Get out of it," he said, trying to sit up.

The kangaroo bounded away to a safe distance. Jax cringed at the pain in his left cheek as he leaned onto his elbows.

"Who are you?" asked a voice. "Why are you here?"

Jax sat up properly, aware that he had kangaroo poo stuck to the side of his shirt. A girl, no older than seventeen, crouched nearby with a long stick held defensively in front of her. She wore navy blue shorts and a clean grey t-shirt with a gold infinity symbol on the front. Messy brown curls fell about her face and tiny freckles smattered her dark skin.

"I asked who you are." Her voice came out like a growl.

"I'm Jax," he said. "Who are you?"

"None of your business. Where did you come from?"

Jax regarded her menacing face and the sharp stick pointing at him. He decided to tell the truth. "From a refugee settlement in New Wulgulmerang."

"Outsiders aren't allowed in here. Why are you here?"

Jax gingerly got to his feet, putting his fingers to his cheek to check how swollen it was. Not too bad. The girl mirrored his movements and stood up straight. She kept the stick trained on him, her face fierce and unyielding.

"I'm not here to hurt anyone," Jax said, "if that's what you're worried about. I just came for some water."

"This is Jindabyne water. Go drink your own water."

Jax almost laughed. "We don't have our own water."

The girl scoffed. "Well that's stupid. Why don't

you make a dam or something instead of trying to steal our water?"

Jax studied her face trying to work out if she was serious or not. "Are you for real?"

"Of course I'm for real." She rolled her eyes and huffed. "We're so sick of outsiders coming in here trying to nick our water supply, all because they're too lazy to build their own dams."

Jax goggled at her as though she was an alien creature. "Is that what people here really believe?" he asked, shock and anger building up inside him. "Have you ever even been outside these walls?"

"Why would I do that? So scavengers like you can rape me."

"I don't know who's been filling your head with all this stuff," Jax said, his voice rising, "but people can't just make dams." He gestured towards the lake beside them. "To make dams you need rivers full of water. And since you've never been outside these walls then I guess you don't know that most of Australia doesn't have access to fresh water."

"Yeah, right. You really expect me to believe that?"

"Look," said Jax, his body exhausted and aching. "I don't really care if you believe me or not. I got little sisters at home and a mum; I just want some water for them. That's why I'm here. So if you'll excuse me, I need to fill up my canisters and get out of here before I lose too much sunlight."

"What if I alert the guards?"

He studied her freckled face, still fierce.

"Then they'll kill me and my family will die."

The stick lowered a few inches and her eyes widened. "They wouldn't kill someone just for taking some water. That would be ridiculous."

"They killed my mate for taking water."

She shifted uncomfortably, her face marred with confusion. "Take your water and get the hell out of here. But this is your one and only free pass. If I see you back here I won't hesitate to dob you in."

Jax filled the canisters and gathered them in his hands as the girl watched. He had another dozen empty canisters in the truck, but he didn't want to push his luck. Hopefully he wouldn't need to come back.

Really, he thought as he climbed back through the wall and walked over to his truck, he'd got off pretty easy. Instead of soldiers with guns he'd only had to contend with a teenage girl with a stick. He didn't think he'd get that lucky twice.

***

His sisters squealed and ran over to the truck to examine the full hydro canisters as soon as Jax pulled up into the yard. His mother put a hand to her heart and almost collapsed in surprise. Jax rushed to her side to steady her.

"This is amazing," she said, her voice catching in her throat as her eyes brimmed with tears. "How did you get them?"

Jax looked away. "It's probably best you don't know."

"Oh Jax," she admonished. "If you risked your life for this, I'll kill you."

"I didn't risk my life, I saved our lives." His mother knew as well as he did that there was a good chance they wouldn't have all survived until the next ration drop.

If they rationed carefully, the water should last them through to the next drop, Jax thought, even with the canisters he would drop off to Ollie the next day at the market as he'd promised.

***

Jax could remember, when he was Nell's age, begging his mother to tell him stories from before the Rise. They had always been his favourite stories—this magical, alien world that existed before he was born. He recalled the ones about the changing seasons. His mother told him of summers spent by the river where she dug her toes into the soft riverbank mud and swam in the sparkling water and once a year her family would holiday by the vast blue ocean. She told him of the autumn when trees turned from green to gold to red. She told him of winters when her parents would drive her up the mountain to play in the snow—a cold, white substance you could mould into funny little men with sticks for arms. She told him of springtime when it rained so much the rivers would flood, everything turned bright green, and colourful flowers bloomed everywhere.

Jax could never picture any of it as a child, or even now as an adult. His seasons consisted of hot and scorching hot. He'd never travelled to the ocean—from the accounts he had heard it was a dangerous place with waves as tall as mountains that gobbled you up. Trees only came in shades of grey and brown and dull green all year round. Sometimes if he looked towards the mountains in the not-quite-so-hot season, at the very peaks he could spot a smallish white patch that his mother told him was snow. On the rare occasions when it rained, the river might gain a trickle, if they were lucky. The grass never turned bright green—the way it had looked at Lake Jindabyne.

This hot season had been one of their worst.

Everyone's crops had suffered. He was not surprised the morning he walked out the back and found Missy, their one remaining goat, laying on her side labouring for breath, her ribcage stark against her fleshless body.

"Don't worry, old girl," he said. "It'll be over soon."

With a heavy heart, he finally did what he should have done months ago and got out his father's shotgun.

Missy wasn't the only one starved from the lack of crops. Jax's family had water for now, but they, too, were starving. And truth be told, though they had rationed their water well, they had resumed relying on government rations more quickly than he had expected. When their hunger couldn't be quieted, everyone started taking extra sips of water here and there in an attempt to stave off the gnawing in their stomachs.

I've got to go back, Jax thought to himself. He just hoped this time he wouldn't be seen by a certain teenage girl with one hell of a right hook. Or someone worse.

CHAPTER FIVE

It did not seem to take as long this time. Maybe it was because he knew where he was going and didn't need to keep consulting his map and compass. Maybe it was because the day wasn't as hot. He hid the truck as he had done before and found the crumbled gap in the wall.

As before, he saw no guards in sight, so he slipped in with his arms full of empty canisters. He got to work right away and was only on his second canister when he heard footsteps approach. He jerked his head around, heart thumping wildly, expecting to see the barrel of a gun. Instead, he received another punch to the face. It didn't knock him out as it had done last time, but he did stumble backwards and trip, dropping the canister he'd just filled and spilling the contents onto the bank.

"I thought I told you not to come back," the girl said. Today she wore a pale purple t-shirt with her navy blue shorts. At least this time she didn't have a stick. She stood with hands on hips and gave him a menacing glare.

"It's been hot. The water didn't last as long as I hoped."

"I still don't see why you don't just build your own dam or something."

"Like I told you," Jax said, sighing, "there's no water to dam."

"You must get water from somewhere."

Jax picked up the canister he dropped. A tiny bit of water sloshed in the bottom. "Yeah," he said, "from here. The government gives us rations."

"Ha!" said the girl, as though this answered everything. "If you get rations, why are you stealing more? Seems to me you're just greedy, taking more than your fair share."

"We don't get enough and people are dying. The people who come here to steal water aren't greedy, they're thirsty and desperate."

The girl frowned, eyeing him sceptically as though trying to work out whether he was pulling her leg.

"The government isn't going to let anyone die, they're the government," she said. "It's their job to look after people. It can't be as bad as you're making it out to be. Like my parents always say, *As long as we stick to the rules we won't run out.*" She crossed her arms and scrunched her nose. "You just aren't careful enough with your water. You use all your rations and then try to take more than your fair share—no wonder they're so tough on scavengers. Maybe you need to stop watering your lawn too much or take shorter showers or something."

Jax screwed up his face. "Lawns? Showers? Are those even real words?"

She huffed impatiently. "Lawns. The grass in your yard, stupid. And showers are how you wash yourself, you know, with water coming through the pipes and sprinkling over your head. What do you call them where you're from?"

"We don't call them anything. Grass is watered by the rain, if we get any, but mostly the ground is dust anyway. And we wash ourselves in the trough outside with water we pump in from the bore. Any water we get from the government is for drinking."

"Are you seriously trying to tell me you have never heard of a lawn or a shower?" She hesitated for a moment, then grabbed him by the wrist and hauled him towards the line of houses. "Come with me."

"I can't go there!" he said, trying to resist her. "If they see me I'm dead meat!"

"My house is that one straight ahead. My parents

are at work. Everyone is at work. No one will see you."

"What about the other kids, like you?"

"Number one, I am not a kid. My name is Daisy and I'm seventeen; eighteen in nine months, so I'm practically an adult, and you don't look like you're that much older than me. Number two, there aren't many kids living here. And definitely none around my age. You know, because of the One Child Policy."

Jax wondered whether his parents had ever heard of the One Child Policy. Somehow he didn't think so.

"Anyway, all the kids are in school right now. I'm already finished with all my exams because I'm in year twelve, so I finished earlier than the others."

Daisy marched him through the white picket gate and swept her arm out to indicate the yard. "Lawn."

If Jax had thought the grass surrounding the lake was the greenest that had ever existed, he was wrong. Here in the yard, where it filled every space inside the white picket fence, the grass was a bright verdant green— a greener green than he could ever have thought possible. And lush! He knelt down to press his hand against it. Unlike the dry prickly clumps of grass back home, this grass was soft and thick. It even smelled different—not dry and dirty, but so fresh he was tempted to eat it like a goat. Daisy tugged him back to his feet before he could entertain the thought, dragging him through the back door into a gleaming kitchen, down a bright hallway and into a tiled bathroom. Against one wall stood a white porcelain tub, not unlike the one in his own family's bathroom, though theirs was old and cracked and they used it for storing old parts of machinery. Daisy let go of his arm and walked over to the tub to turn on a tap set into the wall. Jax let out an "Oh!" of exclamation as water burst out of the round chrome head above the tub. It fell like rain. Jax moved forward to put his hand beneath the flow.

"This is how you wash yourselves?" he asked, amazed. He watched the water hit the bottom of the porcelain tub and run towards the hole at one end. "Where does it go?" he asked pointing to the hole.

Daisy shrugged. "I don't know." She looked him up and down and leaned forward to sniff at him. "You smell like you could use a shower. I'll get you a towel."

It took her only a minute to return with a fluffy blue towel. She left the bathroom and shut the door behind her.

Jax stripped off his clothes and stepped into the tub. The water flowed over his body, washing away the dust and sweat. Though he enjoyed the water running over his skin and cleansing his body, it felt wrong. Back home, people were dying of thirst, yet here at Lake Jindabyne they were wasting water on 'showers' and 'lawns'. How much water had run down the hole while he stood there washing himself? How many hydro canisters would that be?

Jax shut off the water, dried himself and put his clothes back on. The clothes felt rough and dirty against his clean skin. He couldn't remember the last time he had felt so clean, or if he'd ever felt that clean.

He navigated his way down the long hallway and found Daisy in the kitchen eating something long and orange that crunched when she bit into it.

"What is that?" he asked.

"A carrot," she said. "Don't tell me you don't know what a carrot is either."

"Of course I know what a carrot is," Jax replied. "I've just never seen one like that. Our carrots are white and scraggly, that's all, not big and orange like that."

Daisy opened a strange, shiny, white cupboard that held all manner of foods. A waft of cold air came out of it. She pulled out another orange carrot and tossed it to him. Jax bit into it with a crunch. It tasted similar to the carrots they grew out in the vegetable patch, except it was juicy and crisp.

Daisy watched him curiously as he ate it.

"Is it really that bad out there?" she asked. "Is there really no water?"

Jax nodded as he swallowed.

"Wow." She shook her head. "I actually still thought you were lying until I saw your face when I turned on the shower and then the way you bit into that carrot. But it's true, isn't it? I had no idea. I feel like everything I've been told is a lie."

"Me, too," said Jax. "I had no idea this place existed—that people lived like this. How many people live here?"

Daisy shrugged. "About fifty families, I think."

"Who decides who gets to live here?"

"I don't know. The government, I suppose. The people who live here either work at the water facility or are government officials. My parents work at the facility."

"I just can't believe everyone here is using water like it's nothing, while people are dying out in the settlements."

"We have restrictions," Daisy said, defensively. "Like, you can only take five-minute showers and you can only use the sprinklers on the lawn after dark."

Jax laughed humourlessly. "If you could only see how we live you would understand how crazy that sounds to me."

"I wish I could see outside these walls. I want to know what it's like out there."

"Aren't you allowed out?"

Daisy shook her head. "Not without permission

and definitely not if you're a kid. It's not safe out there. It's not just the scavengers, either. With all the bushfires they don't want anyone outside if one starts. Better to stay safe inside the walls."

Jax couldn't help but agree. "They're right, it's not safe out there. Unless you live in a community like New Wulgulmerang, you'd have a hard time surviving. Even then, people are dying all the time. Trust me, stay inside your walls."

Jax might have been reading her wrong, but he could have sworn Daisy looked disappointed.

Talk of the wall reminded Jax of something he had been curious about since he had arrived. "There aren't any guards. I thought there would be guards."

"During the day there are only guards at the front gates," Daisy said. "There are patrols at night who walk the perimeter. I guess they figure no one would be stupid enough to come during daylight hours when it would be easy to get spotted from one of the houses."

Jax flushed red. "I thought you said no one was home during the day."

"Well, scavengers don't know that, do they?"

Jax couldn't help but think how stupid and reckless he had been. What if there had been a patrol or there had been someone besides Daisy who had seen him from their window. Even knowing how dangerous it was to come here, he had not been careful enough. It was only by sheer luck that he hadn't got himself caught.

"Can I fill my canisters up here?" he asked. "Out of one of your taps? It would be safer than filling them up directly from the lake."

"Probably a whole lot cleaner, too," Daisy said. "I wish I could let you, but water to the houses is tracked with a meter so people are kept accountable for their water use. It might be a bit suspicious if our water meter suddenly jumped up its reading within a short space of time. My parents would get in trouble and I would probably be grounded for life. Not that I have anywhere to go really, except to Aisha's house, but she's a few years younger than me and likes listening to old pop music, so I don't go there unless I'm really bored." Daisy pulled a face to show what she thought of Aisha's taste in music.

"I'm not even going to ask what pop music is," Jax said as he made for the door. "I have to go before it gets dark. I'd better get down to the lake and start filling up my canisters before the patrols come out. Thanks for the shower."

Daisy ran up to him and grabbed hold of his arm. "If you ever come back, will you come see me again?" She blushed. "It's just, I don't often get to talk to people my own age and I want to know more about what it's like out there."

Jax studied her freckled face. "As long as you give me some more of those carrots," he said.

Daisy grinned. "Deal."

Jax wondered if he would ever come back. This place was like something out of a dream, but the idea of coming back scared him. The constant reminder that people were wasting water while his family barely clung onto survival… it made him angry. Really angry. And angry people did stupid things. Better to stay away and try to forget what he had seen.

He left Daisy in her shiny, white kitchen and went back to the lake to fill all the canisters and load them into the back of the truck. Jax hoped the old vehicle could handle the extra weight. As he filled the last of the canisters, he looked back towards the houses, a soft breeze ruffling his hair and carrying the scent of something sweet. Definitely better to stay away and forget about the place altogether.

***

Trying not to think about Jindabyne proved more difficult than Jax had anticipated. As he helped his mother prepare dinner, chopping up the withered white carrots he had grown up with, he tried not to think of the way Daisy's orange carrot had crunched when he bit into it, or the juicy flavour that burst in his mouth. Every time they ate their pitiful meals of stringy vegetables he struggled not to think of Daisy's gleaming kitchen, that magical cold cupboard full of food. But he craved to taste that sweet ambrosia once more. It became an obsession. Jax daydreamed about using water to grow a vibrant garden—as vibrant as Daisy's green lawn—to give extra life and flavour to their vegetables. Then he would scold himself for almost giving into temptation. With every passing day the desire grew stronger, until it was the only thing he could think about. It would only be so long before something would tip him over the edge. That something ended up being Nell.

CHAPTER SIX

"Mum! Jax! Come quick!" screamed Yara. She came running up to the yard as fast as her skinny thirteen-year-old legs could carry her.

Jax and his mother stood quickly from where they had been planting seeds in their dusty vegetable garden, hoping for a new crop of sweet potatoes.

"What's wrong, Yara?" asked their mother, wiping dirt from her brow.

"It's Nell," Yara panted, breathless from running. "She collapsed and I can't wake her."

Jax and his mother sprinted after Yara to a spot down by the old tree stump in the eastern paddock. Nell lay on the hard ground like a rag doll, her chest barely rising and falling and her breath coming out in little wheezes. Jax scooped his sister's frail body up in his arms and rushed her inside the cool, dark house. Their mother busied herself dampening a cloth with bore water at the sink to place over her daughter's forehead.

"Yara, grab a canister, she needs water," she ordered.

Yara came back within seconds, holding a canister in two hands and struggling with the weight of it. Jax tipped Nell's head back and opened her mouth while his mother gently trickled water down her throat.

They sent for Doctor Rajesh, who confirmed what Jax had suspected.

"This girl is weak and dehydrated. The dry heat has exacerbated her asthma. She is awake now, but keep her drinking as much water as you can spare. And if you can, boil some water in a pan, get her to put her head over it with a towel covering her so she can breathe in the steam. It will help open up her airways."

He shook his head solemnly as he left, and Jax was sure he heard the doctor mutter about 'dark times'.

"Don't worry about rationing the water for her," Jax said to his mother. "Give her as much as she needs."

"Tell me you're not going back there? It's too dangerous, Jax."

"It'll be fine. I know when the guards are there and I have a friend on the inside. I'll be in and out quick."

She bit her lip, but nodded.

***

"So you came back," Daisy said.

Jax had been thinking about Daisy a lot since he left Jindabyne, as much as he had tried not to. She filled his dreams and waking thoughts, at times more tempting than the prospect of a garden full of carrots and a lake full of water combined. But despite being glad to see her again, the urgency of his sister's situation took precedence over a silly crush on a girl he had only met twice.

"Can you not sneak up on me like that?" he said, from his crouched position by the water's edge. "I thought you were a soldier about to put a bullet in me."

"You really should be more aware of your surroundings."

"Keep a lookout for me then?"

"Why should I? I still don't know if you were telling me the truth. Maybe you really are just a greedy scavenger. For all I know you just told me that big sob story so I wouldn't dob you in."

Jax stopped filling the canister in his hand to look at Daisy. She stood with crossed arms and a raised eyebrow.

"You believed me before, why so sceptical all of a sudden?"

"I had time to think about it."

"Or maybe you just don't want to believe it," said Jax, shaking his head. And if he was honest with himself, he couldn't blame her. He wouldn't want to believe it either if he lived in this paradise. Ignorance was bliss.

The sound of a helicopter grew loud and close. Jax's heart thudded wildly as he looked up at the sky to see it coming to land on the other side of the buildings.

"I know that chopper ," Jax said, relaxing when he realised it wasn't a helicopter full of soldiers coming to apprehend him. He recognised the lettering above the Australian coat of arms that adorned the side of the helicopter: HYDRO-AID. "That's the chopper that brings us the hydro canisters."

"I've seen them loading the canisters," Daisy said. "I've seen them wheeling them out from storage by the pallet-load and stacking them on that platform underneath. I don't know why you think you don't get enough water. You get plenty of water."

"I can assure you we don't," Jax said, resuming filling the canister. "Those canisters have to be shared out between everyone in the whole community. Probably other communities, too. It doesn't last long in this heat. Anyway, I don't have time to convince you I'm telling the truth. My little sister isn't well and I need water quickly. You can either believe me and stand lookout or not believe me and go dob me in. Either way, I'm going to fill these canisters and get out of here."

Daisy didn't move.

"What's her name?" she said after a few minutes.

"What?"

"What's your sister's name? The one who's sick."

"Nell."

"What's wrong with her?"

"Her asthma gets bad sometimes. Plus she's badly dehydrated like we all are."

"How can you have a sister? Your parents should have got sterilised after their first child. It's the rules."

Jax screwed the lid on the full canister and looked up at her. "It might be your rules, but it's not ours. I have four sisters."

"Four sisters!" Daisy stared at him, wide-eyed. "Don't you think that's a bit irresponsible considering how bad you say it is out there? Wouldn't it be better to have less mouths to feed and share water with?"

Jax picked up the next canister and began filling it. "We don't exactly have the means to sterilise people out in the settlement. I'm sure my parents tried to be careful, but I guess they weren't very good at it."

"Four sisters," Daisy murmured under her

breath.

"It's been nice chatting, but I've got to get this water back for Nell," Jax said, scooping up his canisters.

"Is that all you're taking?"

Jax shrugged. "I don't have time for more today, but I'll come back. Unless you plan on turning me in." He gave her a questioning look.

Daisy looked at him as though taking stock. "I'm not saying I believe you yet, but I'll let it slide."

"Thanks."

Jax started back towards the wall.

"Hey," Daisy called out after him. "Next time I'll be your lookout."

Next time. Jax couldn't help but smile.

***

Nell slowly recovered. Within a week the doctor said she could return to building humpies and playing hopscotch as long as she didn't over exert herself. Jax started making regular trips to Jindabyne for water and Daisy's original hostility towards him turned into friendly chatter as she stood lookout. She wanted to know everything about New Wulgulmerang and life outside the wall. Their routine became so regular that Daisy would wait for him by the wall when she knew he would be coming. More often than not, she would insist on dragging him up to the house and they would talk in Daisy's pristine kitchen as she prepared him food.

In the back of his mind Jax knew they were getting careless. He knew he should just get in and out quickly, and that they weren't keeping watch as well as they should be. But he found himself wanting to spend more and more time with Daisy. Besides, he had yet to see a single soldier. It was all so easy.

They should have been more careful. They should have kept better watch. They shouldn't have wasted time splashing water at each other and laughing, drawing attention to themselves, while filling up the canisters. But they did.

As Jax drove off with a truck loaded with canisters, smiling as he remembered the way Daisy had laughed and the way she shook the water from her hair, he had no idea that everything had changed.

CHAPTER SEVEN

Jax arrived outside the wall mid-morning. He took deep breaths of that fresh, almost wet, air. Birds warbled in the trees nearby. Puffs of white cloud floated across the sky high above the wall. In the distance, menacing grey-black clouds formed over the mountains. There had been a storm forming back home when he'd left. If they were lucky they might actually get some rain. As Jax reached his usual entry point, Daisy's freckled nose poked out from the hole.

"You're here," she said, her face splitting into a wide grin. "I almost thought you weren't coming. You're usually here by now."

Jax smiled back. "My sister had an asthma attack this morning, I had to make sure she was okay before I left."

"But she's okay now?"

"She was making a pain of herself teasing Annika when I left, so I'd say she's back to her regular old self. You want to help bring in some canisters? I need a big load this time."

Daisy's grin fell. "How come?"

"Ollie—the guy who told me how to get here in the first place—is low on canisters, so I need to get some for him, too."

She frowned and she bit her lip nervously.

"What's wrong?"

"Things have changed," Daisy said at last. "Someone reported a water thief last time you were here. I guess they must have come home during the day and spotted us filling the canisters. They've tightened security. Guards are patrolling the lake day and night."

Jax groaned and cursed inwardly. "Did the person who reported us recognise you? Did you get in trouble?"

Daisy shook her head, sending her brown curls bouncing about her face. "No, I don't think so. At least no one ever came to reprimand me. They mustn't have seen my face and just thought I was another scavenger."

Jax ran a hand through his own jet black hair. "What will I do? I can't go back empty handed."

"Come back to my house. Mum and Dad are out on their boat doing some fishing and won't be back for hours."

"But what about the guards? Won't they see me?" Jax asked, thinking of the open expanse of grassland between the wall and the row of houses that was clearly visible from the lake.

Daisy's face brightened again. "You actually came on the perfect day. It's a holiday here today. Everyone is out on the water. The whole place is crowded with people. You'll blend right in."

"Won't they know I don't belong?"

"The guards won't have a clue. None of the guards live here in the community, they come from outside, from some sort of military station. They rotate shifts. As long as you look like you belong and they don't see you stealing water, they won't give you a second glance. And everyone else will be too busy enjoying their holiday to notice an extra person."

Daisy took the canisters and pushed them under a nearby scrubby bush, then she grabbed his hand and dragged him inside the wall. Jax noticed how warm and soft her hand felt—not like his own rough, calloused hands. It felt nice, and he didn't want to let go.

This time, instead of the noise of insects and birds, Jax was hit by the sound of voices and laughter. At the lake's edge, there were no kangaroos munching grass against a peaceful backdrop, instead groups of people crowded near the water's edge. Children ran around in brightly coloured underwear with inflated yellow rings on their arms. Swaths of checked material had been spread out on the riverbank containing baskets filled with food. Some of the people sat with poles that had long threads attached like spider's webs reaching into the water. Strange contraptions floated on the water's surface with white sheets billowing in the wind. The enticing smell of cooking meat wafted in their direction causing Jax's stomach to grumble. Daisy tugged him along, skipping and shooting him cheeky grins. Jax spotted men and women in beige uniforms at intervals around the lake, straight-backed and serious, easy to tell apart from the colourful, laughing people enjoying their holiday. None gave him a second glance as he and Daisy made their way up to Daisy's picket fence.

Once inside her gleaming kitchen, she poured him a glass of water—clear running water straight from the tap with not a hydro canister in sight. Jax had so many questions swimming around in his head he didn't know what to ask her first.

"What's the holiday for?"

Daisy looked at him like he was stupid. "Jindabyne Day, of course."

Jax raised a quizzical eyebrow.

"Oh, I guess you wouldn't know about Jindabyne Day. It's the day the community officially opened. We celebrate it every year with a holiday. *A new community, a new hope.* That's the slogan. Do you have a New Wulgulmerang Day?"

"We don't really have many holidays," Jax said hesitantly. When life revolved around survival each day, it was hard to find reasons to celebrate. "Oh!" Jax's face brightened. "We do have Christmas, though. The girls and I find the biggest branch we can and set it up in a pot and make decorations. Mum cooks a nice meal—as nice as she can with what we've got, anyway. She has spices she saves especially for Christmas. We sing and say all the things we're grateful for."

"Yeah," Daisy said, her eyes bright, "we have Christmas, too." She hesitated, as though she wanted to ask something else.

"What is it?" asked Jax.

"Do you... do you have presents?"

"Of course," Jax said with a grin. "We all make each other something. Or sometimes if I have something worth trading, I go down to the market and see if anyone has any toys or books. How do you celebrate Christmas?"

"It's really not much different. A bigger tree, a fancier meal, more gifts, I guess. But at its heart it sounds the same."

"What were those things on the water? With the white sheets attached?"

Daisy giggled. "Those are boats. The white sheets are called sails."

"That's where your parents are? You said they were on a boat."

Daisy nodded.

"What were those poles on the bank?"

"Fishing rods. To catch fish. Don't you use fishing rods to catch fish? Oh." Daisy looked sheepish. "That's right, no water. Sorry."

Jax knew what fish were, of course. There were a couple of traders who brought them back from their travels to the coast. Jax had eaten fish many times before, and he knew that they came from the water, but he didn't know how they were caught.

"How do the rods work?"

Daisy launched into a description and recounted some of her more memorable fishing escapades. Her eyes glinted and her nose scrunched up a little when she was excited. Jax's eyes lingered on her mouth as she spoke. Without fully being aware of what he was doing, he leaned forward and kissed her. He didn't know what possessed him to do it and he expected her to jump back in surprise—maybe even knock him out with a punch to the jaw like she had done the first time they met. He wouldn't have blamed her if she had punched him.

She didn't, though. To Jax's great surprise, Daisy kissed him back. Her hands wrapped around his neck and she drew her body closer as their kiss deepened. Jax didn't know how long they stayed melded together like that—time did not exist inside that kiss—but finally, at some point, they pulled apart, breathless and flushed.

"I've always wondered what it felt like to kiss someone," Daisy said with a huge grin. "It was even better than I imagined."

"You've never kissed anyone before?" Jax asked, his heart still beating wildly in his chest. While girls his age were scarce in the settlement, there were enough for him to be no stranger to the world of kissing.

"I told you, there isn't anyone else here around my age," Daisy replied. She bit her lip shyly and tilted her head to the side. "You wanna do it some more?"

Before he could answer, she started for a door to the left and beckoned Jax to follow her.

Her bedroom was neat and plain—a pallet of whites and browns. The only burst of colour was a canvas on the wall with splashes of bright paint in no discernible pattern. It reminded him of splashes of water, if water happened to be orange and purple and magenta. Daisy sat down on her plain white bedspread and Jax sat beside her. She reached a hand to touch his cheek and ran her fingers along his jawline. He traced the freckles on her nose. They leaned in and their lips met.

Somewhere in the house a door clicked open.

Daisy and Jax broke apart, lips tender and bodies warm with each other's heat. The sky outside had darkened—Jax must have been there for hours.

Daisy gasped. "My parents are back." She looked around frantically. "Stay here in my room. They shouldn't come in. I'll be back after dinner."

Jax looked up at the ceiling as Daisy closed the door behind her, and felt a pang of guilt in the pit of his stomach. Back home, his family waited for him to bring back the next truckload of water, and here he was—in a house out of some sort of dream—kissing a pretty girl. It had been so easy to become lost in this other world, so far removed from his own life. He had to remember why he came here. He had to get water for his family. No more distractions, no matter how pretty and soft that distraction happened to be, and no matter how fast she made his heart beat inside his chest. This was not his world.

As the sun sank out of view on the horizon, Jax knew there would be no chance of him going back tonight. Even if the solar truck made it all the way home without the sun to keep the engine running, darkness also meant that guards would be patrolling the lake against scavengers like himself, with no people around to camouflage him or his intentions. First thing in the morning he would set off. That gave him the whole night to figure out a way to get past the guards. He just hoped his mother and sisters could get by until then.

***

An enticing smell wafted into Jax's nose and his stomach gave a growl. His eyes fluttered open to find Daisy standing by the bed with a plate in hand. Outside, the sky was now pitch black. He must've dozed off for a while.

"I thought you might be hungry," Daisy said, as Jax sat up and rubbed the sleep from his eyes.

Jax's stomach gave another growl in response. He accepted the plate. Brightly coloured vegetables surrounded a whole cooked fish. He dug in, barely savouring the wonderful, full flavours as he wolfed it down to quieten his stomach. Daisy watched him in curious silence. When the plate had been licked clean, Daisy took it from him and put it aside. Jax regretted eating it all and wished he had saved some to take back for his family.

"Thanks," he said. "Will your parents notice it's missing?"

Daisy shook her head. "They got a good catch at the lake today. I told them I was really hungry because I had forgotten to eat lunch and they said I could have seconds. I asked if I could eat it up in my room. They both had work to do in the study, so they didn't care."

Jax marvelled at the idea of asking for seconds and her parents thinking nothing of it.

"What do we do about the guards?" he asked.

"I've been watching them every day since they started the patrols and keeping track of them. Just after nine, once everyone starts work for the day, they have a shift change. The outgoing guards meet the incoming guards up at the northern gates so they can do a debrief or something. It usually takes them about half an hour before they come back down to the southern wall to patrol. We should be safe to get your water then."

It was better than Jax had hoped. He could fill at least half the canisters in his truck in that time, maybe even more if he was quick.

They looked at each other in awkward silence, a whole night of waiting ahead of them.

Daisy smiled and rocked on her heels. "What do you want to do while we wait?"

Jax knew exactly what he wanted to do. He reached out and grabbed her hand so he could pull her in close.

CHAPTER EIGHT

Jax opened his eyes to the twitter of birds outside Daisy's bedroom window. Early morning sunlight filtered through a slight gap in her beige curtains falling across his face like a ribbon of warmth. He moved to get up and Daisy's eyes fluttered open.

"Breakfast?"

Jax nodded.

Daisy's voice carried from the kitchen as she chatted with her parents. By the time Jax had pulled on his clothes, she had returned with a plate full of freshly toasted bread slathered in some sort of lumpy orange spread. On biting into it he discovered the lumpy substance was sweet and sticky and reminded him of the jam his mother made when they picked blackberries from the brambles down in the gully. But this jam had a different flavour and texture to the stuff he was used to. If he was to give it a name, he would have said it tasted like a sunny day tempered by a southerly breeze.

"I wish I could take some of this back to my family," he said between mouthfuls, wondering if every delicious food here came in hues of orange. "The girls would love this."

"You can!" Daisy said, sitting up straight. She had been resting her chin in her hands watching him eat with interest. She had some sort of fascination with watching him eat and he didn't know whether it was because she liked looking at him or whether she was examining him like a creature she had never seen before. "Once my parents leave I'll pack you a bag to take back with us. You can pick whatever food you like."

Jax frowned. "Us?"

"I've been thinking about it a lot—every time you come here. I want to come with you. I want to know what it's like at New Wulgulmerang"

Jax swallowed the mouthful he'd been chewing. "That's a bad idea, Daisy."

"Why?" she said, bristling. "You don't want to spend more time with me? You just want to see me on your own schedule? Or is it that you don't want me to meet your family—you're ashamed of me?"

"Shhh," said Jax, aware that Daisy's parents were downstairs. "That's not true at all. You have no idea what it's like out there. It's nothing like here. You'd never survive."

"So you're calling me weak?"

Jax sighed, running a hand through his hair. "I'm not saying that. But it's best if you stay here."

It hurt him to say it, but he didn't know how to make her understand.

Daisy balled her hands into fists, her fingernails digging into the palms of her hands. "I'm so sick of people telling me what to do. Where I'm not allowed to go. No. I want to see. I want to understand. I can handle it."

Jax studied her determined face, her puffed out chest and clenched fists. "You know," he said slowly, "I think you probably could handle it. I think you're crazy to want to leave this paradise, but somehow I don't think I'd have much hope of stopping you coming."

"No, you wouldn't," Daisy replied, crossing her arms across her chest as her face softened. A half grin pulled at her mouth and Jax knew that the matter had been settled—Daisy would be coming with him whether he liked it or not.

Perhaps he could change her mind before he left.

The front door closed.

"They're gone. Let's go quickly. We don't have much time until changeover." Daisy grabbed a bag from her wardrobe and they headed to the now-empty kitchen to fill it with all manner of foods, many of which Jax had never seen before in his life. He stood in awe as Daisy grabbed stuff off the shelves in the pantry and shoved it into the bag.

"Let's go," she said, zipping up the bag and pulling the strap over her shoulder.

They moved into the backyard and looked over at the water's edge. A thick mist hung over the lake, kissing the water with the soft caress of a lover. The roos had returned, black silhouettes against the white mist. Now that the crowds of people had gone, they had reclaimed their patch of paradise. Daisy pointed out two uniformed figures walking away from the lake towards the northern gates. As soon as their backs retreated out of sight, Daisy and Jax hurried to the wall to retrieve the canisters from where they had stashed them beneath the bush. White mist may have sat above the water, but dark clouds loomed on the horizon. Jax prayed they would bring rain and not just thunderstorms, though he didn't know whether the clouds would even reach his settlement. He sucked his finger and put it in the air to test which way the wind was blowing, but amongst the trees he could not gauge it.

The kangaroos scattered as Daisy and Jax approached, but after realising these two lone people posed no threat, they soon resumed their nibbling. Daisy got to work quickly, filling the canisters, while Jax moved the truck nearer to the hole to make loading easier. He returned to the lake's edge with another armload of canisters. They'd barely filled half the canisters before Daisy bit her lip and looked in the direction of the north gates.

"We don't have much time. The new guards will be here soon."

"Just one more armful of canisters," Jax said. If Daisy really insisted on leaving with him, it wouldn't go unnoticed, and he imagined the security would be even tighter the next time he tried to get back into Jindabyne. He needed to make the most of this trip.

They had barely got the lid on the last canister when they heard the shout. The kangaroos were quick to bolt, bounding away at top speed as two guards ran towards the lake. Jax and Daisy stood momentarily frozen, arms loaded with canisters. Daisy's brain clicked into gear first.

"Run!" she screamed.

Jax pounded after her towards the crack in the wall, trying not to drop any of the full and heavy canisters. The unencumbered guards would be faster, but there was some distance between them yet. As they squeezed through the crack, a sinking feeling settled in Jax's stomach. The guards would now know his entry point and he doubted it would be possible to come through the same way again. This was possibly the last water he would ever steal.

They made it to the truck and loaded the last of the canisters in haphazardly. There was no time to secure them properly. Jax jumped into the driver's side. Daisy climbed into the passenger seat and looked at him beseechingly, but there was no time to argue.

He turned the key in the ignition. The engine coughed and died. He tried again. Nothing.

"Hurry!" cried Daisy.

Jax looked over his shoulder to see the guards emerging through the wall behind them. Sweat beaded on his forehead as he tried a third time, hoping that the dark clouds forming overhead had not obscured the sun too much to render the solar panels useless—that the panels had enough energy stored to get them out of there. The engine revved and spluttered to life. Jax put his foot down hard on the accelerator.

As they sped off along the dirt track towards the old bitumen road, Jax heard the loud bang of a gun being fired.

But it was too late. They were too far away now

for the bullets to hit them.

Jax looked over at Daisy to check she was okay. She wore a big grin like she was going on an adventure and, with a sinking feeling, Jax realised she truly had no idea what she was in for.

CHAPTER NINE

It was hotter than the previous day, despite the dark clouds above them and the wind that bent the trees along the road. Daisy reached for the canister sitting between them and took a few big gulps.

"Go easy," Jax warned. "That has to last us both the whole trip."

"You have a truck full of canisters," she said, rolling her eyes.

"Yeah, and it's got to last my family until the next ration drop."

Daisy shrugged. "You can go back to Jindabyne anytime. We know the guard's routine."

Jax glanced over at her in disbelief. "You don't get it, do you?" he said. "They've seen how we get in. It won't be that easy in the future. And the more often I go back, the more I risk getting caught. That was a close call back there."

Daisy didn't seem to have a reply to this. Instead she leaned back in her seat and sat quietly, thinking.

The further they drove, the drier the landscape became.

"It's so brown," Daisy commented.

The road followed the path of an old riverbed, that had probably been flowing with water once upon a time, but now was rocks and dust.

"Do you think that the dam used to flow into this river?" Daisy asked. "Before they blocked it all off?"

"I guess so. The river leads all the way up to the dam."

Lightning cracked in the distance and several seconds later thunder boomed, but the clouds didn't release a single droplet of rain. Jax shifted uncomfortably in his seat. With the grass so dry, one strike of lightning would be like flint striking against steel and one spark would have the whole bush ablaze.

After a while Daisy fell asleep beside him, her head lolling to one side. Jax let his mind wander to home, wondering how Nell was holding up. Thunderstorms always made her asthma worse. The canisters clinked and rattled in the back over each crack in the bitumen. He hadn't got as many this trip as he had planned, but how safe would it be to return?

And then there was Daisy. He glanced over at her sleeping form, her dark curls bouncing as the truck hit each bump. He would have to take her back to Jindabyne. He should never have allowed her to come with him in the first place. What would happen when her parents realised she was missing? Jax imagined armed guards showing up at his door to retrieve Daisy, then putting him in front of a firing squad for kidnapping and water theft. His gaze rested on her serene face, her long dark lashes, her slightly parted lips. What had he been thinking letting her come along? Not that he had much choice. He couldn't leave her there with the guards chasing them. They might have shot her on the spot for helping a water thief.

He turned his eyes back to the road and let out a strangled yell as he slammed his foot onto the brake. Too late. The truck collided with the herd of feral goats that had wandered into his path. There was a sickening crunch. Both Jax and Daisy lurched forward as the vehicle came to a halt. A cascade of metallic clangs told Jax that half the canisters had just fallen out the back of the truck. Goats dashed into the trees on either side of the road, bleating and screaming in fright.

"Are you okay?" Jax asked Daisy, as he rubbed

his chest where it had collided with the steering wheel.

Daisy nodded, now fully awake and wide-eyed. A red welt had appeared on her cheek where she had hit it on some part of the vehicle. "I'm fine. What happened?"

"Goats," Jax muttered. He undid his seatbelt and climbed out the door to see how much damage had been done to the front of his truck. The matted furry body of a brown goat lay bloody on the road, half under the front chassis. It made no sound or movement, not even the rise and fall of shallow breathing. The front of the truck wasn't too bad, though. A broken headlight and a bit of a dent, but the bull bar had taken most of the impact.

"Help me move the goat from under here," Jax instructed Daisy.

Daisy shuddered and recoiled.

Jax rolled his eyes. "Come on. It's dead, it's not going to bite. I need you to help me. It will be quicker if we do it together."

Daisy stepped tentatively forward and bent down to grab the goat's front legs. Its dead, blank eyes stared up at her and she turned her head away. Jax took hold of the back legs, and together they dragged it out from under the chassis. Once it was out, he instructed Daisy to help him lift the goat into the back of the truck.

"Why exactly are we taking a dead goat with us?" Daisy asked as they heaved the body into the truck amongst the remaining hydro canisters.

"Why pass up good meat?" Jax said. "As long as it has no disease, it'll provide us with a few good meals."

Daisy made a face, but said nothing further. They set to work reloading the fallen canisters back into the truck, taking care to seek out any that had rolled away into the scrub and shooing away a couple of goats who had climbed on top of them. Jax made sure the canisters were all secured and immovable in case they ran into any further obstacles along the way.

"I've never seen anything dead before," Daisy said quietly as they climbed back into the truck. "I mean, obviously I've seen dead fish before, but this is different. So big and… bloody."

Jax turned the key and blew out a breath of relief when the truck started on his second try. "You'll see a lot more dead things before the day is out. It's hard to avoid death out here."

Daisy shrunk down in the seat. Jax wondered if she was finally realising what she had got herself into by coming along.

Daisy did not fall back to sleep for the remainder of the drive, but nor did she talk as she had done the first half of their journey. She sat in silence, staring out the front windscreen. Jax had been right that she would see more death before the day was out. They passed dead wombats on the side of the road with their four stubby legs stuck up in the air and tongues hanging out. They passed dead cockatoos with feathers askew. They passed skeletons of creatures big and small. Most would have died of thirst trying to find non-existent water sources.

The sun was high in the sky when the truck rumbled into New Wulgulmerang, and here Daisy sat up a little straighter in her seat. She peered out the window in open-mouthed shock at the ramshackle buildings and the skin-and-bone people dressed in dusty clothes. Jax knew that to Daisy it must be just like entering an alien world—the same way he had felt the first time he'd stepped inside the walls of Lake Jindabyne to see those pristine houses all in a row. He pulled up to his family's property. Without unloading the truck or even waiting for Daisy to disembark, Jax sprinted inside the house. He had been gone for far longer than he had planned and he needed to let his family know he was okay. He also wanted to see how Nell was doing. The house was silent except for Jax's footsteps. Something felt wrong.

Instinctively, he ran full pelt down the hallway to Nell's bedroom.

They all stood silently around Nell's bed: his mother with her frail frame and limp dark hair falling about her shoulders; his sister Marn, who now stood the same height as their mother, her legs too long for her old blue dress; Yara, all knobbly knees and freckled arms, standing uncharacteristically still apart from a silent shuddering and heaving of her shoulders; and little Annika, whose head rested on the pillow next to Nell's, rivulets of tears running down her grubby cheeks.

Jax's heart stopped. Nell's body lay still and pale atop the blankets. And like the goat he had hit with his truck, there was no rise and fall of Nell's chest.

"Noooo!" The scream wrenched from his throat—from somewhere inside his soul. He punched the door frame so hard he tore the skin from his knuckles. "No, no, no!" He punched the wall over and over, welcoming the pain as red blood bloomed there.

"Oh Jax," his mother said, taking him in her arms like she had done when he was small. "When you didn't come back yesterday I thought I had lost you both."

"I'm sorry. I'm so sorry," Jax said, his body trembled. Any moment his legs would give out beneath him. "If I had been back sooner—"

"No," his mother said, firmly. "It wouldn't have made a difference. The doctor said…" She sniffed, squeezing him tightly. "He said there was nothing we could do. No amount of water could have saved her. Her body just failed. It's the way of the world these days." She took a deep breath. "Death is inevitable."

Behind the strong façade she held together in

front of her children, Jax could see the brokenness and pain in her eyes. Somehow that made it worse. Why should they have to accept death as inevitable? Death should not be inevitable for a nine-year-old girl.

"NO!" Jax screamed.

He turned and fled from the room, knocking into Daisy who stood in the hallway just outside the door.

Daisy. This would never have happened to Daisy or to any of those government workers at Jindabyne. He glared at her as he pushed past, and she recoiled from his anger.

They didn't have to contend with pithy water rations and scrawny vegetables. *They* didn't have to contend with death around every bend. He kicked out at the door as he burst outside into the sweltering heat.

It wasn't fair. How could those government officials live in that paradise, thriving, when the people in the settlements, were dying from thirst and hunger? How could they use water to have showers and water grass, while giving out meagre rations that barely kept the people alive? Jax screamed and swore, kicking fence posts and tearing branches from trees. He raged until he stumbled from faintness and his legs gave out beneath him. His body shook. He squeezed his eyes shut in the hope he might be swallowed up by the darkness.

Gentle hands pushed a metal container to his lips

and he gulped down the water gratefully. Daisy slumped down next to him as she screwed the lid back onto the hydro canister. Jax felt a slight flame of embarrassment heat his face at his outburst. He should have held it inside like his mother. He was supposed to be strong, like his father. But the vision of his sister's pale face penetrated every corner of his mind.

Daisy rested a soft hand upon his rough one. "Your sister just died; you're allowed to be angry."

"I'm angry at you," he said, the rage still swirling inside him, fighting to burst forth.

"Me?" She flinched in shock, but did not remove her hand from his.

"You and everyone who lives at that place."

Daisy lowered her eyes. "I truly didn't realise how bad it was out here. You must think we're selfish, gluttonous monsters."

"You don't even know the half of how bad it is."

"I want to see everything. I want to know." She reached out to touch him.

He shook away her hand from his shoulder. "Just go home," he said, turning away from her. "Go back to your paradise."

"Jax—"

"I said go!" he yelled. "Don't you get it? I don't want you here reminding me that if Nell had been born into your family instead of mine she would still be alive."

Daisy stood without a word. Through his haze of anger, he saw a tear splash down her cheek before she turned and left him sitting there in the dirt.

How long he sat there, he had no idea. What did time matter anyway? It must have been hours later when Annika came to find him and curled up in his lap. The sky had turned a dusky blue and the first stars appeared. Jax rested his cheek against Annika's fine dark hair.

"Are you thirsty?" he asked her, his voice cracked and dry. What was he saying? They were always thirsty.

She looked up at him with brown eyes that were too wide for her tiny face. He squeezed her hand and tried to offer her a small smile through his tears—he hadn't even realised he'd been crying.

"I brought back water," he said.

"I know," Annika said. "Daisy unloaded it already."

"She did?" Jax said in surprise. "Is she still here?"

Annika nodded. "She gave us special food, too, from her bag. She's really nice. I like her. Can she stay?"

Jax kissed Annika's forehead. "We'll see."

He stood up, stiff and sore and covered in dust, picking up Annika to carry her back to the house.

He found Daisy in the kitchen helping his mother carve up the goat from the truck. Her face was lined with grim determination, but Jax could see her hand shaking slightly. She looked up as he entered the room.

"Can I talk to you?" he asked.

Jax put Annika down and Daisy wiped the blood off her hands on a rag. Together they went outside to sit on the front porch.

"I know you want me to leave," Daisy said. "And I will, I promise. But I can't really get back on my own, so I thought I'd do what I can… to help."

"You don't have to leave," Jax said. "Not yet. I do want to show you what life is like here."

"I'd like that," Daisy said, reaching out and taking his hand. This time he didn't shake it off.

"I need to do things here. I need to help my mum arrange a funeral for Nell." His voice caught in his throat. "Then I'll show you. I'll show you everything."

CHAPTER TEN

The funeral took place under the big old gum up the back paddock. Jax worked all morning in the blazing heat to dig a grave beside his father's. The weather-worn rock, with his father's name etched into it, stood tall and proud. He'd yet to find the perfect rock for Nell to mark her final resting place—how could he when he still couldn't accept she was truly gone? He wouldn't let Daisy or anyone else help him dig—it was something he wanted to do on his own. Guilt and anger and despair all fought to dominate his mind. He poured each thought and emotion into his arms and into each shovel full of dirt, as though he could toss them aside as easily as the earth. But no amount of digging could shift them.

Friends and neighbours came to pay their

respects as Nell's little body was lowered into the ground. They told stories of Nell's endless energy and bright smile, of her mischief and resilience. Jax tried to smile and laugh along with them, but inside he felt hollow. He wanted to tell the story of how Nell had helped him build a seesaw and swing from scrap for Annika the Christmas after his father died, and how Annika had cried because Nell was so proud of it she didn't want Annika to play on it in case it got broken. He wanted to tell the story of how Nell, though often loud and full of trouble, could also be sweet and quiet, like when their father had been ill in bed and she read stories from the old storybook that had belonged to their grandmother and had been lovingly saved when their parents escaped the Rise. But he did not share these stories because talking about Nell in the past tense meant Nell was as dead as their father and Jax was not ready to accept that.

Some of their friends and neighbours brought food to share, and though no one had much to spare, their generosity knew no bounds. At one point Jax paused to wonder how Daisy felt about the food as it must have seemed inadequate compared to what she was used to. But Daisy did not complain or even give a hint that she felt this way. When Jax sought her out amongst the crowd of people at the wake, she was graciously carrying around a plate of something she had prepared from the supplies she'd packed from her house, offering it to everyone and not touching a thing for herself.

***

In the intervening days, Daisy proved an invaluable help and support to Jax and his family. She helped with the chores and made sure they remembered to eat and drink, always at their elbow with a hydro canister or plate of interesting foods from what Jax's sisters referred to as "Daisy's Magic Bag". Nell would have loved that magic bag and all the goodies that appeared from inside. As the initial wave of grief ebbed somewhat, and the haze of his stormy thoughts lifted, Jax could fully appreciate Daisy's constant tender help to this family of strangers in their time of need, so far removed from the life she was used to. In the back of his mind, he was still waiting for the knock on the door to take Daisy back. She must have missed her parents, but she didn't say anything.

Jax approached her as she cleared weeds from the dry garden beds out the back. She looked up at the sound of his footsteps and smiled as she wiped the sweat from her forehead with the back of her hand, leaving a dirty streak there. Even covered in dirt, she was beautiful.

"I haven't been to see Ollie since I got back," Jax said. "He's the one who gave me the map. I need to take him some hydro canisters. Want to come? I can show you around."

"Of course!" Daisy stood and brushed some of the dust from her knees.

They walked along the dirt road that led from Jax's house to the market. It was usually only a twenty minute walk, but they walked at a casual pace. In one hand, Jax pulled a cart behind him with the canisters for Ollie and with the other he clasped Daisy's hand.

At the market, Daisy wanted to examine each stall with wonder. Jax did his best to answer all her questions—"Where do they find all these odds and ends? What kind of vegetable is that? Can anyone set up a stall?"—but in the end he had to tug at her hand or they would never have reached Ollie.

Ollie sat huddled on an old wicker chair behind the counter, his eyes half-closed as he caught a nap between customers. He appeared scrawnier than Jax had last seen him, his wrinkled skin clinging to his bones.

"Ollie," Jax said.

Ollie didn't wake. A pang of fear cut through Jax's stomach.

"Ollie," Jax repeated, louder.

Ollie grunted awake and focused on the two people standing in front of him. "That you, Jax?"

Jax sighed, his stomach unclenching. "This is

Daisy. We brought you some more hydro canisters."

Ollie raised an eyebrow at Daisy, then looked back to Jax and shook his head. "I heard what happened to lil' Nell. You keep 'em for yerself and yer family."

"You need water, too." Jax tried to hand the canisters to Ollie, but the old man crossed his arms.

"I don't need 'em no more."

"Of course you do!" Jax said. "Look at you. You're nothing but bones and your skin is dry as a dead lizard. I got it for you. Take it."

"I'm tellin' you, I don't need it no more." He coughed a dry, hoarse cough. "If you can't tell, it's over fer me."

"Don't be stupid," Jax said, perplexed. "If you're not well, that's exactly why you need to take the water."

"We're all gonna die, kid. I'm just gonna go sooner rather than later. What good's water to a dead man? It's those young'uns that need it. Keep it for yer family." He closed his eyes and bent his head to his chest, ignoring Jax pleading with him to at least take one canister. A minute later, soft snores vibrated from the back of his throat. Jax could not tell if the old man was faking it or if he had really fallen back to sleep. Either way, he took it as a sign that Ollie would not be accepting any hydro canisters today.

As they walked back through the stalls, Jax kicked

at the dirt, sending up clouds of dust. Daisy wasn't as interested in the stalls now and instead bit her lip, lost in thought.

"I wish I could take you all back with me to Jindabyne," she said with a sigh. "You and your family and Ollie and…" She looked at the ragged people behind the stalls, the skinny children playing a game in the dirt under a scraggly tree, the pitiful vegetables for sale. "And everyone."

"I'm sure the government would love that." Jax laughed humourlessly.

"We have so much water there. Enough to share. I just wish we could get it here somehow."

"I can only bring so much back in the truck," Jax said. "It would never be enough for everyone."

Daisy sighed again. "What if you had a bigger truck?" she suggested.

"From where? And how would we be able to load a whole truck between the guards' shifts?"

"You could do it over several days. Stay with me at the house."

"I can't be away from my family that long. Not again. And it will only be more dangerous next time I go back. Who knows if I'll even be able to get any next time. Besides, won't your parents put you on lockdown when you get back?"

They hadn't discussed how Daisy's parents would react to finding their only daughter missing—presumably kidnapped by a water thief. Jax was still surprised government agents hadn't rocked up to his front door to retrieve her and shoot him on the spot. Daisy twisted the bottom of her shirt and avoided eye contact with Jax.

"What?" Jax asked.

"They won't have noticed me gone."

"How could they not notice?"

"I left a note that I had gone to stay with my friend Aisha overnight. And they're on night shift the rest of the week, so they'll be asleep during the day and assume I'm asleep when they go to work. I barely ever see them on night shift weeks. I'm practically an adult now, so they know I'm fine looking after myself."

"What do your parents do, exactly?" Jax asked.

Daisy shrugged. "They're engineers. They do improvements on the dam when needed. Repairs in the control room, check the flood gates are in working order in case the dam gets too full to make sure it doesn't overflow, make sure the filtration system is functioning properly. Stuff like that."

"Wait, back up." Jax stopped and looked at Daisy wide-eyed. "The dam has flood gates that can open."

"Of course," said Daisy. "All dams have flood gates."

"Do those flood gates open into the river? The one we drove along to get here?"

"I guess so," Daisy said, then her eyes widened, too, as she realised what Jax was getting at. "You want to open the flood gates?"

"Think about it. Before the dam was built, where did all that water go? If the flood gates are opened the water would flow down the river like it is supposed to. It would flow all the way down to New Wulgulmerang." The idea grew in Jax's mind quickly and his excitement grew with it. This was the answer. It had to be. "You mentioned a control room. Is that where you would go to open the flood gates?"

Daisy shrugged. "I guess so. The control room controls everything, I think."

"How easy is it to get into the control room? And do you know how the floodgates work?"

As Jax's excitement grew, Daisy looked more and more uncomfortable, but she continued to answer questions. "I've been in there with my parents before. I could lead you there no problem. As for how the floodgates work, my dad is forever going on about dam stuff—I think I might be able to figure it out. Maybe."

Jax took her hands, excitement buzzing through him like their old generator gone haywire.

Daisy's face did not reflect the excitement he felt.

"What's wrong? You don't think the plan will work?"

"It's just… if we do this…"

"What?" prompted Jax. "If we do this, we could save a lot of people."

"I know, it's just…"

Jax waited, keeping his grip on Daisy's hands.

"Look," she said at last. "I know this sounds really selfish, and I do want everyone here to have water, too, but I can't not think about how it will affect everyone back at Jindabyne. Opening the dam, sending the water down the river… what if there's not enough left for us?"

Jax took a deep breath, picturing the huge, sparkling lake at Jindabyne. "If you don't want to help I'll understand, but I have to do this. I have to bring water to New Wulgulmerang."

"I want to help," said Daisy. She stood a little straighter as a look of steely resolve replaced the apprehension in her eyes. "After everything I've seen here… Well, it's not fair is it? Everyone should have water. We'll just have to learn to wash ourselves less and let our lawns turn brown. I would feel guilty for the rest of my life if I knew people were dying of thirst just so I could take a shower."

Jax squeezed her hands in gratitude. "Tell me more about the control room."

***

Jax found his mum in Nell's room, standing as though she'd turned to stone.

"Mum?"

"I swear I could hear her laughing," his mum said, her voice cracking slightly.

Jax came up behind her and wrapped his arms around her shoulders. "She had the best laugh."

"Wicked, I used to call it," she said, placing a hand over his. "That girl was always up to something."

Jax buried his face in his mother's dark, coarse hair as he had done when he was a little boy, breathing in the smell of earth and woodsmoke from the stove.

"You're going back, aren't you?" she said. It was a statement more than a question.

"How did you know?"

"I figured you'd have to take Daisy back eventually, but mostly because I can feel it in the way you're hugging me right now. It feels like a good bye."

"I'll be back, I promise."

"You can't guarantee that. Every time you go I sit here waiting with heart in throat not knowing if I'll see you again. It's too dangerous. I can't lose you, too. I've already lost too much."

"I know. That's why I have to go. Daisy and I have a plan. We're going to make everything better. No one else has to die."

She pulled away from him and whipped around to face him, her eyes wide and terrified. "Whatever it is, don't do it! We'll survive. We always do."

"No, we don't! Nell didn't survive. Dad didn't survive. I'm not going to let the same thing happen to Marn or Yara or Annika or you."

Tears wavered in his mother's eyes.

"I'll come back," Jax said. "I promise."

"You're so much like your father." She pulled him into her arms and squeezed him tight, then whispered in his ear, "Go."

"Thank you, Mum."

"You better come back in one piece."

"I will."

CHAPTER ELEVEN

The old truck bumped along the road towards Jindabyne. In the distance to the east, several plumes of smoke rose into the sky to blend with the dark clouds, though it was too far away to see any hint of flame. Thunder had rumbled and lightning flashed all night as Jax lay in bed going over their plan, almost like a warning. Not a drop of rain fell. At least the fires burned far enough away that they wouldn't come close to New Wulgulmerang, so long as the wind didn't pick up too much.

"I just realised something," Daisy said. "I haven't seen a single vehicle on the road, except for us."

"It's getting harder to get parts," Jax said. "Besides, it's not like there's anywhere to go. Outside the settlements there's nothing. Do people at Jindabyne have cars? I've never seen one there."

"Well we're not supposed to leave, are we?" Daisy said with a shrug. "We do get the army trucks come in for the soldiers to changeover. They come from somewhere up north, I think." She took a deep breath as though steeling herself up to say something, but she stayed silent. After a few moments, she took another deep breath and said, "You don't have to come with me. It only needs one person to change the input in the system. My father has bored me with talking about dams so many times, I'm pretty sure it's just a matter of fiddling with the levels on the computer and I can do that on my own. Plus it would be easier if I did it by myself, that way we don't have to sneak you in." She bit her lip as she glanced at him to gauge his response.

Jax knew logically she was right. It made sense for her to do it alone. She was the one who knew her way around and knew how to work the floodgates. He was unnecessary to the plan and they were more likely to be caught with both of them there.

But he had to follow his gut.

"I need to be there," he said. "I need to do this."

"Wouldn't you rather stay with your family? Your sister just died. Stay and grieve."

"I don't want to grieve," Jax said, his fists tightening on the steering wheel. "I want to do something so I don't have to lose anyone else."

"What about your mum and your sisters? I bet they don't want to lose anyone else either," Daisy reasoned. "This could turn into a suicide mission if we get caught."

"I know." He heaved a sigh. "But I just can't stay there. I can't keep thinking about Nell. It's too hard. Walking in to see her little body lying there like that… I just felt so helpless, so powerless to have prevented it. At least this way I feel like I'm doing something, you know, so maybe it won't feel like Nell's death was in vain."

***

They arrived at dawn, as planned, and parked the truck in its usual hiding place. They had predicted that the crack in the wall would be blocked, but the two armed guards standing by the opening still made Jax's stomach sink. They would have to rely on Plan B. Or even Plan C.

On the surface, Plan B appeared to be a solid plan, but there were so many things that could go wrong. This plan involved entering through the front gates. Daisy would tell the guards who she was and one of her parents would come identify her so she could be let back in. Once inside, she would go to a door to the north of the gates that was used by scientists to collect samples from flora and fauna outside the wall. Daisy would unlatch it from the inside and let Jax in.

It sounded simple, but everyone would know Daisy had been outside the wall, which was forbidden. She would be in big trouble, and even Daisy wasn't sure what the punishment would be. At the very least, her parents might insist on not letting Daisy out of their sight. Worse, the guards might question her and could connect her with helping the water thief who had escaped just days before with a girl who looked an awful lot like Daisy.

Plan C was less risky, in some ways. They would hide near the northern door for the next scientific research team to come through, and try to slip inside unnoticed. Unfortunately, Daisy didn't know how often the research teams went out and it could be days before the door opened. Even then, the possibility of sneaking through seemed a bit far-fetched. In the end, they decided to risk Plan B.

Jax watched from a safe distance, hidden behind a line of trees, as Daisy approached the gate. The glint from unseen guns in the watchtowers made Jax want to shout out at her to come back. What if they shot first and asked questions later? But the guns remained silent. Jax stayed just long enough to hear the shout of a male voice telling her to "Stop". Just long enough to see Daisy raise her hands above her head and two guards escort Daisy inside. All Jax could do now was trust that Daisy would be okay—trust that they would retrieve her parents to confirm her identity and that they would simply give her a warning and let her go.

CHAPTER TWELVE

It was quite a hike through the bushland to get to the northern door. Wary of snakes and the possibility of being spotted by researchers who could be roving around outside the wall collecting samples, Jax remained hypervigilant. He paused after every couple of steps, listening carefully for a shout of discovery. As Jax finally reached the door Daisy had described—a plain grey door set so unobtrusively in the concrete wall that he almost missed it—he let out a sigh of relief. Now to wait.

Jax checked his watch. It was not yet ten o'clock. He'd got the watch several years ago as a gift for his dad, trading some old parts from a tractor he'd found down in a gully. The trader had told him that a lot of the watches he found were useless because they ran on batteries and batteries were too hard to come by, but this watch worked by winding the little knob on the side.

Jax touched the knob lightly, a grim determination flowing through his veins. After his father had died, Jax's mother had carefully removed the watch from his wrist before the burial and presented it to Jax. It reminded Jax of his father… and of how little time people had on this Earth. He thought of Nell and clenched his fists. He refused to anyone else die. Daisy's plan had to work.

Time ticked by and Daisy did not come. Dark clouds rolled in over Jindabyne and lightning crackled as it had done the previous night as he contemplated their plan. He hoped it wasn't a bad omen. Jax leant against a tree, wishing he had brought water with him as sweat trickled down the side of face.

Minutes turned to hours. Had they been questioning her all this time? Daisy planned to tell them that she'd only been outside for a few hours, rather than the days she'd really spent in New Wulgulmerang; she'd simply been curious and wandered out the gap in the wall, then freaked out when she tried to get back in and had seen the guards. Had her parents put her under twenty-four-hour watch? They'd talked of the possibility, but Daisy didn't think her parents would actually do it. She'd been so sure they'd just give her a stern talking to and then return to work.

The sun rose to its apex, then started sinking lower in the sky, casting long shadows where it peeked out between the storm clouds. Each boom of thunder set Jax on edge. He didn't want to be stuck out in the bush if the lightning hit close by and started a fire. A black snake slithered past, but did not bother Jax. A mob of kangaroos came to graze amongst the trees and he wondered if they were the same ones from the lake free to roam inside or outside the wall as took their fancy—not stuck inside as prisoners like Daisy, nor treated like trespassers to be shot on sight like Jax. His leg started to cramp, so he stretched it and flexed his ankle. If Daisy didn't come, he'd have to revert to their other plan. Once night fell he would return to his truck and camp there the night. He couldn't stay where he was with no water or shelter. The truck had a half full hydro canister and a blanket at least.

A click and a creak interrupted his thoughts. The door opened slowly. Jax made sure he was well hidden behind the towering gum and stood stock still, listening for the whistle Daisy would use to signal to him if it was safe. It didn't come. Instead, he heard a murmur of voices and the crunch of two sets of feet. Jax leant into the tree, willing himself to blend in with his surroundings. He hoped that it was a research team and not armed guards.

If they had connected Daisy to the water thief and questioned her until she cracked, maybe they were coming put him to death as they had done with Tavai. Jax dared not breathe. As they drew closer, their voices carried. A man and a woman.

"Petra said she spotted a new hive up near Devil's Landing," the woman said. "We should scout the area for bee activity."

The man made a sound in his throat that sounded like agreement. Jax relaxed slightly. Definitely researchers. Maybe the plan would work after all.

The scientist's footsteps crunched through the dry twigs to Jax's left and off through the bush. Jax peeked around the tree at the door, but of course the researchers had closed it behind them. He hoped they'd left it unlocked so they could to get back inside. He crept over to the door and gently tried to turn the handle, but it refused to budge. Damn. Jax scratched the stubble on his chin. The scientists must have a key to get back in; he would just have to take it from them. With a sinking feeling in his stomach and thoughts flying around his head of how this could all go very, very wrong, Jax headed in the direction of the two researchers.

It didn't take him long to catch up. He moved as silently as he could out of sight, trying to match his footsteps with theirs so he didn't give himself away. Their chatter helped mask any noise he was making, as did the constant rumble of thunder. The ground sloped downwards through thick scrub into a small valley that might have once been a stream.

"I'll search the left, you search to the right," the woman said to her colleague.

The man nodded and veered off into the trees flanking the right side of the old stream bed. Jax followed the woman as she veered in the opposite direction, rationalising that the woman—being much more petite in stature to the man—would be easier for him to overpower. *Good Lord, I'm thinking like a criminal.*

The woman scanned each tree and bush intently and slowly. She would be easy to sneak up on, Jax thought, so engrossed as she was. He wouldn't hurt her, he just wanted the key. He did want more distance between her and her partner, though, so there would more time for Jax to get away before he came running to her aid. As Jax readied himself to make his move, the woman did something surprising. Her face changed from serious to excited.

She placed her clipboard down on a nearby rock along with her pen, then started removing everything from her body that hung loose: her bracelet, the string of beads she wore around her neck, her lanyard with her ID card. And the set of keys clipped to her belt. She placed them all on top of her clipboard, just a few metres away from Jax.

"Should have brought the ladder," she muttered, before swinging herself up into the tree.

Jax couldn't believe his luck. As soon as the woman was well into the branches of the tree, Jax crept forward and picked up the keys as gently as he could to avoid them jangling and making noise. A flash of lighting lit the darkening sky, followed by a loud boom of thunder that caused Jax to jump and almost fumble the keys. He looked furtively towards the woman's back, but she had not noticed him. For extra measure, he also took the woman's ID and slipped it around his neck. As long as no one looked at the photo, from a distance it might make him look official—as though he belonged there.

"Hey, what are you doing?" the woman yelled.

Jax whipped his head up to see the woman looking straight down at him. He froze.

"Mike!" she called out in the direction of her colleague, her voice echoing through the bush. "Hey, Mike, there's some kid here, he's nicked my keys." She started descending from the tree.

Damn. Jax's brain kicked into gear. He unfroze and ran, ignoring the branches that caught his clothes and scratched his skin. As long as he reached the door before the two scientists caught up with him he might stand a chance. Until they alerted the guards to the presence of an intruder anyway.

Lightning forked across the sky ahead. The wind had picked up blowing up dust and leaves. Trees bent and bowed around him. Jax skidded out of the way of a branch as it cracked as loud as the thunder and fell. His hands shook and his heart pounded in his chest.

When he arrived back at the door it was still closed, with no sign of Daisy anywhere. He fumbled with the keys until he found one that slid easily into the lock and turned. With a deep breath, he opened the door a crack and peeked through to make sure no one was on the other side. The coast was clear beyond the door, but behind him the scientists burst through the trees.

"Stop right there, kid," the man ordered. "That is private property, you can't go in there."

Without hesitation, Jax slipped through the door and slammed it behind him, clicking the lock in place, leaving the two scientists standing on the other side. If the male scientist had his own set of keys, Jax was done for. If not, they would need to make the trek to the front gates, which would buy Jax some time.

A cold, white corridor met him on the other side of the door and Jax had no idea which way he should go. Daisy was the key to getting to the control room—Jax was lost without her—but he had no idea where to even start looking for her. The only thing he knew for sure was that her house lay south of where he now stood. His heart thudded loudly with every step he took down the deserted corridor. The door behind him remained closed, giving him hope that the scientists had been forced to go to the gates instead, but any moment another person might appear and recognise him as a stranger.

A door opened up ahead, but Jax had nowhere to hide in the empty corridor. All he could do was walk with purpose and pray the ID card on the lanyard would fool them. Two women came out of the door, deep in conversation about numbers and statistics. Their voices and clacking high heels echoed off the walls as they marched straight past Jax, barely sparing him a glance. Jax's breathing returned—he hadn't even realised he had been holding it. He quickened his pace, determined to get out of there before he came across anyone else.

At the end of the next corridor there was another door—this one had a glowing green 'EXIT' sign above it. Touching his watch for good luck, he pushed through the door and breathed a sigh of relief.

Everywhere he looked, grey concrete buildings stood crammed together—official looking buildings with placards on their doors and aluminium-framed windows where he caught glimpses of people seated at desks. Others hurried back and forth between the buildings with clipboards in hand. Jax blended in with the crowd as he navigated towards the houses he could see in the distance. Once out of sight of the bland concrete buildings, he broke into a sprint, desperate to find out what had happened to Daisy and get on with their plan. Though the façades of the houses all looked almost identical—aside from the occasional personalisation of strange little ceramic bearded men in the garden or a tyre hung from a tree by a rope—Jax soon found the one he was looking for. There was a little wooden plaque on the front door that read 'Home Sweet Home', but Jax did not go in through this door, instead he slipped around the back where there would be less chance of being spotted.

The back door opened easily. Inside the house, Jax detected no movement, no sound of voices or footsteps, just the gentle hum of the big white food cupboard. He tiptoed in the direction of Daisy's bedroom, listening carefully for any signs of people. The bedroom was empty. The whole house was empty. Neither Daisy nor her parents were anywhere to be seen.

Jax sighed, contemplating whether he should attempt to get to the control room on his own and follow through with their plan. However, it was useless without Daisy, he would be going in blind. He sat down on Daisy's bed and ran a hand through his hair. Outside the booms of thunder came closer together as though foretelling his impending doom. It wouldn't be long before the guards were alerted to the presence of an intruder. He didn't know what else to do but—

A blaring siren sounded throughout the house.

CHAPTER THIRTEEN

The sirens infiltrated every part of the room, vibrating the floor beneath Jax's feet. He ran to Daisy's bedroom window and pulled aside the curtain a fraction so he could peek out. People ran back and forth with serious expressions and determined strides, shouting things that Jax couldn't understand through the closed window. The sirens weren't just coming from within the house, but all around the walled community. Leaving the house now would be suicide.

He sat back down on the bed and put his head in his hands. It had all gone terribly wrong. He knew there was a chance he would get caught—more than a chance, it was practically inevitable—but he had hoped they would at least get to the control room first and carry out their plan. At least then it would have been worth the risk—his death would have meant something. Worse still, he had pulled Daisy into this mess.

The front door banged open and Jax tensed. Running footsteps pounded inside. The footsteps stopped briefly here and there and doors opened and shut. They were searching for him. Jax contemplated hiding—under the bed or in Daisy's wardrobe—but what was the use? They would find him anyway and he didn't want to be found cowering. He was man enough to accept his fate with courage. He stood up and waited. The bedroom door swung open and Jax jutted out his chin. However, it was not a soldier who entered, but a teenage girl with tangled brown curls and a freckled nose.

"Jax!" Daisy said as she leapt into his arms to hug him tight. "I hoped you got in and would be here."

Jax kissed her forehead and cheeks, then finally a lingering kiss on her lips. When he pulled away he asked, "What happened?"

"The guards called for my parents. I thought I was in big trouble, but they let me off with a warning. Mum and Dad were furious, though. They made me stay with them at work so they could keep an eye on me. Then the sirens went off. There's a fire on the western side, outside the wall. Nearly everyone has gone to fight it before it takes off and gets out of hand. My parents told me to go home and stay there. I couldn't check the northern door because they have the whole place on lockdown." She looked at him with wild eyes. "I was so scared you were still out there."

"It's okay, I got in," he said, smoothing his hand over her curls. "Wait, the sirens are for the fire? They're not for me?"

"Definitely the fire siren," Daisy said. "I've heard it enough times in my life to be sure."

Jax relaxed the tension he'd been holding in his body. "So what do we do now?"

At that, Daisy's face brightened. "Actually, it's perfect! Everyone is distracted by the fire. If we go now, there's less chance of being noticed in all the chaos."

***

People ran back and forth around them as Jax and Daisy pushed their way towards the grey building closest to the lake. Some people shuttled children towards the houses, others had donned bright yellow jackets and red helmets and darted towards the gates. None noticed an out-of-place stranger in their midst, so focused as they were on the fire threat. The sirens stopped howling, and as the sound faded, the air was filled with a cacophony of voices shouting and children crying.

Daisy cursed as they reached the front door to the main facility. "All the external doors must have been locked in the shutdown." Then her eyes lit up as she looked at Jax. "Hey, pass me that key card."

Daisy grabbed the ID card from Jax and inserted it into the slot in the door to unlock it.

Jax watched in amazement. "I had no idea it could do that."

They slipped inside. The halls were dark and silent except for their echoing footsteps as Daisy led the way towards the control room. She tried the key card once more when they reached the control room door. This time they were not so lucky.

"Wrong department," Daisy said, pushing against the door in frustration. "I wish I had my mum or dad's card, theirs would have worked."

"So how do we get in?"

Daisy bit her lip and looked around. "The locker room. Maybe someone left a key card there in their hurry to evacuate from the building."

They hastened down the corridor to a small room with metal lockers lining one wall and coat hooks for bags and jackets on the other.

"These are all locked," Jax said, pulling on the door of the closest locker.

"Check the pockets on the jackets."

Jax pulled a key card out of the third pocket he checked. "Found one."

"What's the code in the top corner?"

"SCI."

Daisy shook her head. "That's science department again. We need engineering or technical support or even a manager."

They rustled through every pocket, finding pens and handkerchiefs and even some nuts and bolts. Jax's hands fumbled and his heart raced, wary as he was of their limited window of time. They had no way of knowing when the lockdown would end and people would return to the building. If the lightning had only caused a small blaze that could easily be contained, then they needed to act fast. And what about the scientists? Had they been distracted by the fire, or had they had time to alert the guards of an intruder? Beads of sweat formed on Jax's brow. Finally his hand closed around another card.

"MGR," he read aloud.

"That should do it."

Daisy exited the locker room ahead of Jax, then turned around quickly, pushing Jax back inside.

"What is—"

"Shhh," said Daisy, pushing Jax around the corner towards the jackets.

Then Jax heard the tell-tale murmur of voices—it looked like the building wasn't as deserted as they had originally thought. Once the voices had passed, they crept back along the corridor towards the control room. Thirty seconds later, they had to slip into some sort of meeting room and hide under a giant table until another lot of footsteps had passed. By the time they made it back to the control room their nerves were completely frazzled. Jax's nails dug into his palms as Daisy tried the key card. He let out an audible sigh of relief when it worked and the door clicked open.

Inside the room, panels lined the walls with levers and buttons and computer screens. Little lights flashed. Whirring and beeps punctuated the air. On one wall small screens showed black and white images of the dam outside. Jax had never seen anything like it and stared around at the control room agape. It was as though someone had taken all the random pieces in Ollie's hut and assembled them together like a jigsaw puzzle then brought it all to life. Daisy headed straight to the computer screens to study them.

"I think if I fiddle with the water levels it should open the floodgates," she said.

"You think?" said Jax, his voice raising an octave as he turned towards her. "So you're not one-hundred per cent certain? I thought you said you knew everything about this control room."

"I don't know *everything* about the control room, I've only picked up bits and pieces over the years."

"You said you've watched your parents working in here loads of times." Panic rose inside him.

"I have," said Daisy, "but I've never actually seen them open the flood gates before. It's supposed to be for when the dam gets too full, but that's never happened in my whole life. I'm sure I remember Dad saying it had to do with the water levels."

"Try it," Jax said, trying to calm himself. "See if it works." He rubbed the face of his watch absent-mindedly, praying their plan would work. At the same time, it seemed impossible to believe that they could actually send water down the old, dry riverbed towards his home. He could imagine the surprised looks on everyone's faces when water came flowing into New Wulgulmerang.

Daisy had barely touched the computer, when the door to the control room swung open.

CHAPTER FOURTEEN

A portly, balding man in black slacks and a crisp white shirt entered through the door. He visibly jumped at the sight of the two teenagers inside the room.

"What are you doing in here?" he demanded. "Everyone who is not out fighting the fires is supposed to be inside their homes."

"My parents told us to wait here," Daisy lied, stepping away from the computer and trying to look casual. "They had to check on something, then they were going to escort us back to the house."

The man narrowed his eyes at Daisy. "You're Kale and Jamila's kid?" he asked.

Daisy nodded, her messy curls bobbing.

"And who are you?" he asked Jax. "I've never

seen you before."

"He's visiting from Lake Eucumbene," Daisy interjected. "He's training to work at the facility there. They sent him here to learn about the Jindabyne Dam. He's staying with us and my dad's been showing him the ropes."

Jax gave a weak smile and flashed the ID around his neck, taking care to cover the picture. He held his breath, hoping the man would buy their lie. He studied them both for a moment. Jax's palms started to sweat.

"Just don't touch anything," the man said sternly as he turned to leave.

"We won't," Daisy said. "We promise."

He almost got out the door. Almost. "Forgot what I came in here for," he chuckled. He came back into the room and pointed at the key card on the control panel by Jax—the one Daisy and Jax had pick-pocketed. "I must have left it here. Had to borrow Varney's card just to get back in and look for it "

Jax and Daisy leaned against chairs, trying to look casual and uninterested.

"Don't want to lose it," he said as he picked it up. He paused and frowned. "You know, it's funny, I could have sworn I put it in my pocket. My memory must be playing tricks on me." He studied Daisy, eyes narrowing. "I could have sworn I already saw your parents leaving to fight the fires, too. What did you say they had to check on?"

"I'm not sure," Daisy said. "They just told me to wait here."

"Seems strange. I was allocated to do all the last checks so everyone else could go help with the fire. Why would they need to check on anything?"

Daisy shrugged. "You'd have to ask them."

He scrutinised Jax the way Jax sometimes studied a crooked fence post, as though he had just noticed something was not quite right.

"What happened to your clothes?"

Jax glanced down at his pants and t-shirt. Streaks of dirt marred his clothing. A small tear gaped at the knee of his trousers. Prickle burrs stuck to the laces of his boots.

"Oh, um, Daisy's dad took me for a tour of the Lake earlier. I tripped over and got a bit messed up."

The man drummed his fingers against his key card thoughtfully. "I think you should both come with me down to the guard tower. One of the guards can escort you back to your house."

"But my parents won't know where I've gone!" Daisy exclaimed. "They told us quite specifically to wait here. I'm sure they'll be back any second."

"No, I really think it is best you get back to your

house as soon as possible. Your parents will thank me for getting you to safety and they'll be able to get to the fire more quickly if they don't have to worry about taking you home first."

Jax could feel their plan falling apart. If they left this room they would never have another chance to get back in.

Screw it.

Before the man knew what was happening, Jax balled up his fist and punched him in the face. It didn't quite have the same effect as one of Daisy's punches, but the man reeled and stumbled backwards, swearing.

"Do it, Daisy!" Jax shouted.

Daisy dashed to the computer screen and used a finger to start dragging down the bars indicating the water level.

"What the ruddy hell do you think you're doing!" the man shouted, his eyes wide in horror. "You're going to open all the flood gates!"

"That's the point," said Jax.

The man tried to lunge towards Daisy, his face red and furious. Jax blocked him from getting near the computer.

"Do you have any idea what you are doing? We need that water to survive, you stupid kids. This isn't a game."

"It's not a game to me either," Jax replied, side stepping back and forth as the man tried to get around him. "Other people need water, too. My people need water."

The man sneered as he put all his shoulder strength into trying to push past. "*Your* people. So you're from one of the settlements then. I knew something wasn't right about you. Give it up, boy. You can open the flood gates all you like, but as soon as you leave this room they'll be closed up again."

They both stopped and stared at each other, breathing heavily, faces red, eyes blazing.

"Why should you get all the water?" Jax screamed, anger coursing through him so his whole body shook. "Why should you have green grass and plump vegetables and spouts that sprinkle water over you to clean yourselves while we're out there dying of dehydration? How is that fair? Why do you get to control who gets water and who doesn't?"

The man smiled a condescending smile without a hint of warmth. "Because if we don't control it then we *all* die. You people out there are going to die anyway. That environment is not sustainable for life in the long term. The best we can do is create communities like this one and put all our resources into it so at least Australia has some hope of continuing the human race into the future. Communities like Jindabyne are the future of Australia."

Jax felt like he had been punched in the stomach. "Y-you never intended for us to survive."

"Well technically I have nothing to do with it. It's the government who made the decision. I was just one of the lucky ones who happened to have a skillset they needed, just like Daisy's folks."

Jax stumbled back against the control board. "But… they can't do that. They can't just forsake us like that."

"They haven't forsaken you. You get rations, don't you? They could have just left you to die. They still have some humanity."

The rage boiled up inside Jax again. A hot, trembling rage that threatened to gush out of him like the water gushing out of the gates of the dam. He scanned the room for a weapon—the red canister on the wall with the fire symbol and the little hose coming out the top looked heavy. Perfect. He tore it from its holder and brandished it above his head.

"You can't just decide who gets to live and who gets to die. Every person is worthy of life."

The man threw his hands over his head defensively. "Don't kill the messenger. It's the government's fault, not mine. I just work here."

"How are you going with the levels, Daisy?" Jax asked, the canister high above his head.

Daisy stepped away. "That's it. They're as low as they can go. They're all reading one hundred per cent open."

Jax swung the red canister down with all the strength he had. It came crashing down, not on the man's head, but onto the control panel.

He smashed the canister into the monitor, then brought it down onto the keyboard.

"You need to destroy the whole system," Daisy said. "The hard drive. Everything." He smashed buttons and blinking lights and cubes in metal casing filled with wires. The man was too stunned, too frightened to do anything but stand there agape. Jax stopped for just a second to watch the floodgates on the little black and white screens as water poured out of them, then he swung the heavy canister to smash the screens, too.

The man, coming to his senses, pulled a small black device from his pocket and pressed a button. "Emergency code one-one-two. Send any available guards to the control room."

Jax and Daisy pushed passed him, causing him to stumble and fall. The two teens raced out the door and down the corridor. The exit door at the end of the corridor swung open as two guards came bursting through. Daisy pulled Jax into the nearest open door, into some sort of kitchen area, and they ducked down inside. The guards' footsteps thundered passed them towards the control room. They would only have seconds before the bald man told them which way Jax and Daisy had gone.

"Quick," Daisy said, pulling him back out the door.

The door was mere metres away, but that corridor felt as long as the river bed between there and New Wulgulmerang. They burst out into the open air—air that was now thick with smoke. The sun had been blotted out, making it appear a dull pink colour. Everything else looked yellow. Blackened leaves floated about and landed at their feet. They raced towards Daisy's house as fine white ash settled in their hair and on their clothes.

"Hey! Stop!" a voice boomed behind them, then the crack of a shotgun echoed against the buildings.

Jax half expected to feel the sting of a bullet, but no pain came. A warning shot. But they didn't stop, they pumped their legs harder, hand-in-hand, too afraid to let go of each other. As they reached Daisy's house they veered around the side and through to the backyard, temporarily cutting them off from the sight of the pursuing guards. Though neither of them had spoken a word to each other about their destination, they instinctively ran for the same place. Jax only hoped that the fire had diverted the guards.

The sky turned from dull yellow to blood red. It felt as though they had been thrust onto another planet. An eerie quiet settled within the walls. Jax spared a glance at the lake, and maybe it was just hopeful thinking, but he swore it already looked lower.

They had nearly reached the hole in the wall when more bullet shots rent the air behind them. These were no warning shots—the bullets whizzed by them and embedded into the stone bricks, causing grey dust to explode in little plumes.

They were trapped now, with guards on their tails and the possibility of more guards roaming the other side of the wall.

They had no choice but to risk it. Jax burst through to the other side with Daisy close on his heels, heading for the hidden solar truck. There was a single shout of, "Hey!", but it was not until the two pursuing guards from inside burst through that the lone guard on the outside of the wall fumbled his gun into position and joined the chase. There was a series of cracks. Jax weaved left and right, hoping to avoid the bullets.

When Jax and Daisy reached the truck they brushed aside some of the branches hiding it from view and climbed in. Jax turned the key in the ignition. Nothing.

"Why isn't it starting?" asked Daisy, fingers gripping the dash as she looked over her shoulder at their pursuers, who drew ever closer. She squealed as a bullet lodged itself in the rear of the truck.

Jax didn't respond, though sweat ran down his forehead. To his relief, the engine revved the second time he tried, despite the smoke-filled skies blotting out the sun. He put his foot to the floor and the truck burst out of its coverings. Making a decision he wasn't sure was brilliance or madness, he drove into the bush instead of taking the track in hopes any bullets would find it harder to reach their target. The truck bumped over rocks and branches, nearly becoming air borne as Jax avoided hitting any trees. Bullets hit metal with loud twangs. Jax prayed they didn't hit anything important, like a tyre. The passenger side mirror struck a tree as Jax navigated a narrow gap.

"We're losing them," Daisy said, turned around in her seat to look out the rear window.

Jax glanced in his mirror. The three guards were still in hot pursuit, but falling further and further behind. Their bullets weren't even striking the truck any more.

The wind changed and heavy smoke blanketed the bush, obscuring the guards completely. Jax slowed down, wary of not being able to see any oncoming trees through the smoke. The guards would have no hope of catching them now. Unfortunately, the smoke made it difficult to gauge which direction he was driving. He rumbled along at walking pace in the direction he thought the track would be.

"Jax!" Daisy screamed.

But Jax had seen it, too. Flames licking up the eucalypts ahead of them. Jax hit the brakes, then turned the wheel to veer away from the fire. He increased his speed as much as he could in the dense smoke. Embers fell on the bonnet of the truck. Jax turned the knob that worked the windscreen wipers, praying they would work. They squeaked against the windshield wiping the ash build up in a neat arch.

"It's getting closer," Daisy whimpered beside him.

Inside the truck the temperature soared.

Jax eased his foot down on the accelerator, trying to keep the gap between them and the fire from closing. They hit a downward slope and with a bump the tyres hit bitumen. With the road to guide them, Jax accelerated faster. The road continued downhill, meaning a slower path for the flames to follow them.

As they drove, putting distance between themselves and the fires, the smoke cleared enough for the road to be more visible and Jax was able to drive at a faster pace. He didn't think the soldiers would chase after him—at least not yet. The fires would occupy them for a while. Once the fires were out, then they would come for him.

The road wound around the mountain tracks alongside the old dry riverbed. But it wasn't so dry anymore. Already, he could see evidence of their handiwork. For the first time in Jax's memory, a trickle of water bubbled over the dusty rocks as it raced Jax and Daisy towards New Wulgulmerang.

"He was right, you know," Daisy said. "We might have released the water for now, but they'll fix it eventually and they'll just close the flood gates again."

Jax gripped the steering wheel a little tighter. "I know." He heaved a deep sigh. "And even if they don't, how long until the river dries up on its own anyway."

They sat in silence for a few moments, lost in their thoughts of the hopelessness of it all.

"At least it's something," Daisy said. "For now."

Jax looked over at her and she looked back. They both smiled small weary smiles. Jax reached out and took her hand. Behind them smoke plumes blanketed the sky above Lake Jindabyne whilst orange flames engulfed the bush. Ahead of them lay an uncertain future. But beside them the Snowy River gurgled back to life. For now.

ABOUT THE AUTHOR

Jo Hart is a speculative fiction author with short stories published in anthologies and online. Born and raised in rural Victoria, when she is not writing she is busy being a mum and geeking out over all things fantasy. Jo hopes the Drowned Earth series will start a conversation on what a future Australia might look like if we don't take action against climate change.

You can find out more about Jo and her writing at:

Website: http://johartauthor.com
Facebook: http://facebook.com/JoHartAuthor
Instagram: http://instagram.com/jo.hart.author
Twitter: http://twitter.com/gracefuldoe

ABOUT DEADSET PRESS

Deadset Press is the publishing imprint for Aussie Speculative Fiction – a community aimed at supporting Australian and Kiwi authors. You can learn more at:

www.aussiespeculativefiction.com

ABOUT THE SERIES

Drowned Earth is a series of eight standalone novellas, set in a shared world.

Prequel: Shards of Silver by Alanah Andrews

Debbie is on board a ship when an asteroid collides with Antarctica, causing a tsunami. And it's heading her way…
(eBook Only: Free Download)

The Rise by Sue-Ellen Pashley

The great Rise means that resources are scarce and not readily shared. But with her best friend's life at stake, along with some stranded refugees, Katie James knows she must prove there's more to being human than just existing. Even if that puts her on the same kill list.

Fire Over Troubled Water by Nick Marone

Despite winds, torrential rains, storms, and bushfires, a fresh water merchant searches for his lost daughter among the autonomous island communities of flooded eastern New South Wales.

Submerged City by Austin P. Sheehan

Melbourne is under martial law, overseen by general Messinger—an extremist who believes the flood is God's retribution against the left-wing agenda…

Tides of War by Marcus Turner

After discovering a strange man in a row boat, Maria wages war on the lotus cities—clandestine floating communities off the coast of Victoria that are reserved for the wealthy.

The Jindabyne Secret by Jo Hart

With nothing but a map and a rickety solar truck, Jax journeys to the top secret fresh water facility at Lake Jindabyne—one of the few fresh water lakes left in Australia. What he discovers there could be the key to saving his whole community, as long as the government doesn't kill him first.

River of Diamonds by S. M. Isaac

Who would want to leave one of the last idyllic settlements since the Rise? Rosa has a map, a mercenary, and a hope to salvage a future for the world.

Salvaged by C.A. Clark

Cassie lives in the safe haven of academics on the anchored city of new Melbourne. After a diving incident she is rescued by a territorial beach combing gang who trade goods washed up by the frequent storms. Cassie wishes she had never taken her home for granted.

Emoto's Promise by Shel Calopa

Five hundred years after the flood, can Macie defeat the technology which has enslaved the last remaining humans in the walled city of Darwin?

ALSO BY DEADSET PRESS

Annual Anthologies

Beginnings: Australian Speculative Fiction Vol. 1

Journeys: Australian Speculative Fiction Vol. 2

Zodiac Series

Capricorn

Aquarius

Pisces

www.aussiespeculativefiction.com